William A. Smith

On Human Entozoa

comprising the description of the different species of worms found in the intestines

and other parts of the human body, and the pathology and treatment of the

various affections produced by their presence

William A. Smith

On Human Entozoa
comprising the description of the different species of worms found in the intestines and other parts of the human body, and the pathology and treatment of the various affections produced by their presence

ISBN/EAN: 9783337368241

Printed in Europe, USA, Canada, Australia, Japan

Cover: Foto ©Andreas Hilbeck / pixelio.de

More available books at **www.hansebooks.com**

ON

HUMAN ENTOZOA:

COMPRISING

THE DESCRIPTION OF THE DIFFERENT SPECIES OF WORMS
FOUND IN THE INTESTINES AND OTHER PARTS OF
THE HUMAN BODY, AND THE PATHOLOGY AND
TREATMENT OF THE VARIOUS AFFECTIONS
PRODUCED BY THEIR PRESENCE.

TO WHICH IS ADDED

A GLOSSARY OF THE PRINCIPAL TERMS EMPLOYED.

BY

WM. ABBOTTS SMITH, M.D., M.R.C.P. Lond.,

SENIOR ASSISTANT-PHYSICIAN TO THE METROPOLITAN FREE HOSPITAL,
LATE SENIOR PHYSICIAN TO THE CITY DISPENSARY, ETC.

LONDON:
H. K. LEWIS, 15, GOWER STREET NORTH,
1863.

PREFACE.

THE nature of the present work having been sufficiently indicated on the Title Page, it is unnecessary for me to occupy the reader's attention with any lengthened prefatory remarks.

I feel, however, that I cannot permit its issue without recording my deep sense of obligation to Dr. Davaine, of Paris, the author of one of the best modern treatises upon Entozoa,[1] for the disinterested and unconditional manner in which he gave me permission to make use of any portions of his work; and to Messrs. Baillière and Son, the proprietors of the copyright, as well as the publishers, of Dr. Davaine's treatise, for a similar privilege, of which I have, as will be seen upon a perusal of the following pages, largely availed myself.

It also affords me much gratification to express here my warmest thanks to those colleagues and friends who have kindly placed at my disposal numerous facts and cases, having especial reference to the subject of Entozoa.

---

[1] *Traité des Entozoaires et des Maladies Vermineuses de l'homme et des animaux domestiques.* Paris: Messrs. Baillière and Son. 1860.

In the general arrangement of the contents of the book, I have followed the plan adopted by Dr. Davaine, of dividing it into three parts, so as to keep the description of the different species of Entozoa distinct from the pathology and treatment of the affections occasioned by their presence. I have added a short Glossary of the principal terms employed, both with the hope that it may prove useful, and also in order to avoid the frequent repetition of explanatory notes.

38, DOUGHTY STREET,
MECKLENBURGH SQUARE, W.C.
March, 1863.

TABLE OF CONTENTS.

PART I.

SYNOPSIS OF THE ENTOZOA WHICH ARE FOUND IN MAN.

CHAPTER 4.—NEMATOIDEA.

CHAPTER 5.—ACANTHOTHECA.

PART II.

THE PATHOLOGY AND TREATMENT OF HUMAN ENTOZOA.

PART III.

SPECIAL THERAPEUTICS.

ON HUMAN ENTOZOA.

PART I.

SYNOPSIS OF THE ENTOZOA WHICH ARE FOUND IN MAN.

ENTOZOA are parasitic animals which live in the organs of other animals, and which possess neither a distinct respiratory apparatus, nor articulated appendages specially adapted to locomotion.

The entozoa found in man may be arranged into five separate classes, namely, the Protozoa, the Cestoidea, the Trematoda, the Nematoidea, and the Acanthotheca.

CHAPTER I.

THE PROTOZOA, OR INFUSORIA.

THE entozoa included in this class are very minute animalcules, being visible only by the aid of the microscope; they are usually of irregular shape, and

B

have no complete distinction between their different organs. In some the simple organization is reducible to the type of a cell, whilst in others, which are more complex, the functions are still performed by simple organs, and not by special parts.

The integuments of the protozoa are sometimes soft, contractile, and not distinct from the substance of the body; sometimes more distinct, and reticulated; sometimes firm and non-contractile, or hard and horny, and remaining after the destruction of the animal. They are usually provided with various appendages which serve for the purposes of taking food, of locomotion, and possibly of respiration; these are the contractile expansions, sometimes short and broad, sometimes long and filiform, which certain protozoa have the power of frequently emitting or retracting; or, in others, these are the constantly agitated vibratile cilia, and the little filaments which appear to be under the control of the will of the animalcule.

The body is composed of a soft, transparent, diffluent, and contractile substance. One or more reddish vesicles, which appear and disappear at irregular intervals, represent a rudimentary system of circulation. The digestive tube, like the other organs, is usually altogether wanting.

No well-defined limits have, as yet, been assigned to the class of protozoa, both because it is easy to include within this class the larvæ of other animals which are higher in the scale of organization, and because it is difficult to distinguish the protozoa from plants which are endowed with motion, or even from particles newly separated from a living structure, and still showing signs of vitality, as may happen in the case of muscular fibre, of vibratile cilia, of spermatozoa, or of zoospores.

The protozoa are the most widely diffused of all animals. They exist in both running and stagnant, and soft and hard water, in decaying substances, in mosses and confervæ, etc. They soon make their appearance in decomposing vegetable or animal matter; they are found upon the integuments of animals which live in water, and in different organs of the cold, and even of warm-blooded animals.

The protozoa which live in the organs of animals are true entozoa, for they perish quickly when they are removed from these organs; and, on the other hand, infusorial animalcules which are accustomed to live in a free state, perish when they are introduced into an animal structure.

The following are the various protozoa which are known to affect the human subject:

1. *Vibriones.*—These are extremely minute, filiform protozoa, which do not possess any visible organization, nor parts suitable for locomotion; they are multiplied by their transverse division, and move by means of their general contraction. The vibriones are the protozoa which appear first in all infusions, and which, on account of their extreme smallness of size and of the imperfection of our means of observation, must be considered as the most elementary animalcules which are at present known to us. Two genera are included under this head.

(*a.*) *Genus Bacterium.*—The protozoa belonging to this genus are found in various animal fluids when in a state of decomposition, in the white matter which collects about the teeth,[1] etc.

(*b.*) *Genus Vibrio.*—The microscopical parasites belonging to this genus are found in the evacuations of persons suffering from cholera and from diarrhœa, in putrescent urine, and in the purulent discharge of balanitis, and of leucorrhœa.

2. *Monades.*—Protozoa which have a fixed form, either round or oval; their bodies are of a homogeneous appearance, without any distinct integument, and are capable of adherence to surrounding objects; they have no visible intestine nor mouth; one or more flagelliform filaments serve the purpose of locomotory organs.

Three genera of the monades have been observed in relation with the human subject.

(*a.*) *Genus Monas.*—Body naked, of a rounded or oblong form, with variable expansions; possesses a single flagelliform filament. Has been observed in the urine of persons suffering from cholera.

(*b.*) *Genus Cercomonas.*—The body is of a roundish or oval form; it possesses an anterior flagelliform filament, and also a posterior prolongation, of variable length, which is more or less filiform, and sometimes adheres to surrounding objects so as to momentarily fix the position of the animal.

There are two varieties, or species, of the *Cercomonas* found in connection with the human subject.

---

[1] Küchenmeister doubts the existence of the animalcules said by some writers to exist about the teeth, and he thinks that there is some confusion between them and the buccal Algæ, or spores. Ficinus, who gave the name of *Denticola Hominis* to the parasite which is found in this locality, states that he has often met with it, and especially in hollow molar teeth.

Fig. 1.[1]

The first species (marked 1 in the woodcut) sometimes exists in very considerable numbers in the
recent evacuations of persons affected with cholera ;
the second species of the animalcule (marked 2 in the
woodcut) is smaller than the preceding ; it has been
observed in the dejections of patients suffering from
typhoid fever.

(*c.*) *Genus Trichomonas.*—This very minute animalcule is similar in appearance to the two genera
just described ; it differs, however, in possessing an
anterior flagelliform filament, surrounded by a group
of vibratile cilia. The *Trichomonas Vaginalis* has
been observed in the vaginal mucus. Trichomonad
protozoa are often united together in groups composed of about five or six individuals, of which only
the moving flagelliform appendages can be distinguished. When the mucus becomes reduced in
temperature they quickly perish and disappear.

3. *Paramecia.*—Protozoa having a soft, flexible
body, of variable form, usually oblong, more or less
flattened, and provided with a reticulated integument, which is loose, and covered with numerous
vibratile cilia, arranged in a regular series ; each
paramecium possesses a distinct intestinal tube ; the
movements of these animalcules are rapid, and sometimes gyratory.

The *Paramecium Coli* has been found in the
human colon, and in the evacuations.

[1] Explanation of Figure 1.—The *Cercomonas hominis* magnified 350 times. The two varieties are marked respectively
1 and 2.

CHAPTER II.

CESTOIDEA.

THE entozoa which belong to this class are composed of a soft, and usually flattened body; they have no mouth nor intestinal cavity; calcareous corpuscles, ordinarily very numerous, are scattered about in various parts of the body of the worm; there is usually a head (known as the *nurse*, or *scolex*), furnished with two or four little depressions (known as *suckers*), which are muscular and very contractile, and are often armed with hooks, arranged either in a terminal circlet around a small tube (called the *rostrum* or *rostellum*), or in pairs in front of each sucker, or else in considerable number upon four retractile tubes; the body of the worm (called *strobile*) is formed of numerous pieces, or rings; these either remain for a long period continuous with each other and with the head, or are soon detached, and live for some time in a free state, when they are spoken of as *cucurbitini* or *proglottides;* four ramifying longitudinal canals may be observed upon the head and the rings;—these possibly serve the purpose of an excretory apparatus. The embryo is usually oval-shaped, and armed with six hooks, from which circumstance it derives the name of *hexacanthus.* The larva undergoes various transformations, but is sometimes multiplied in the same form by gemmation.

The cestoidea are the most common of all the entozoa. They comprise a very large number of species which, in their different stages, occupy all of the viscera of vertebrated animals. The cestoid worms in man and in the domestic animals belong to two distinct sub-classes, the Tæniæ and the Bothriocephali.

Sub-Class I.—Tæniæ.

These are cestoid worms which have a head (*scolex*), furnished with four suckers, and frequently with a rostellum, which may be either armed with hooks, or not; a body (*strobile*), in the form of a flat band, composed of numerous pieces; these pieces (*cucurbitini, proglottides*) are either joined together or free, and are provided, when they have become adult, with male and female reproductive organs, which are situated near the margins of the rings.

Embryonic Condition :—An oval vesicle, or *hexacanthus*.

Larval Condition :—The hydrated or acephalocyst form; the cystic form (*echinococcus, cænurus,* and *cysticercus*); in the greater number of species the larval form is unknown; the *scolex*.

Perfect Condition :—The *cucurbitinus* or *proglottis*.

In the larval state tæniæ are found exclusively in the parenchymatous organs, or in serous cavities; in the perfect state they only exist in the intestinal cavity of vertebrated animals. They are common in the mammiferæ and in birds, but are very rare in reptiles and in fishes.

The cestoid worms belonging to the sub-class of Tæniæ are propagated by Alternate Generation ;[1] in

---

[1] Besides the reproduction by means of the genital organs, certain animals are also reproduced by germs; in both cases it may

fact, if we compare with one another the embryo, the
head, and the rings of a tape-worm, it may be readily

happen that the individual which is produced does not resemble
the individual which is the producer. It is known that in the
case of batrachian animals, and of insects, the larva which issues
from the ovum does not resemble the parent, but that sooner or
later it acquires the shape and organisation of the parent by
metamorphosis. In the case of some other animals, the individual which issues from the ovum, differing also in form and
organisation from the individual which produced it, does not
become metamorphosed into an individual resembling the parent,
but perishes without ever reaching the adult state; and there are
other individuals to which it gives birth, by means of germs, which
acquire the form of the original parent, and which, in their turn,
produce ova. The individual which has issued from the ovum,
does not resemble, either in form, or in organisation, that which
produced it, nor does it in any greater degree resemble its
progeny; this latter possesses the form of the first parent, or it
acquires it by a metamorphosis. There are consequently two
very distinct phases of generation; but sometimes this second
generation does not arrive at the adult condition, but reproduces
a third, differing from itself and from that which preceded it, and
this third generation alone assumes the type of the primitive
parent.

By the term *Alternate Generation*, or *Digenesis*, is therefore
understood the succession of dissimilar generations, sexual and
non-sexual, after which the primitive type is resumed.

It frequently occurs that an individual belonging to one of
these phases of generation (ordinarily that in which genital organs
are not possessed) produces new individuals similar to itself, and
these, in their turn, give birth to other individuals similar to
themselves before either of them produces individuals of a dissimilar character. These similar individuals, born of a common
stock and successively one from the other, cannot be considered
as constituting new phases of generation, for they do not form a
more advanced stage in the evolution of the animal which they
represent, and they only multiply the individual-stock; the dissimilar individuals, on the contrary, always form a stage in
advance towards the adult state. The larva which produces a
succession of ten or twelve individuals, born one from the other
by gemmation, and similar to each other, has not definitively ten or

seen that they constitute three distinct individualities, of which one, at least, is derived from another
by gemmation.

The head, or scolex, evidently possesses a special
individuality. It is distinguished from each of the
rings by its form, by its suckers, by the constant
absence of sexual organs, and often by the presence
of hooks ; and, if in certain species, it seems to
belong to the series of rings because it is not plainly
separated from them, the separation is well-marked
in other species ; besides which, the head of certain
cestoid worms has been seen detached, and has even
been described as a distinct animal under the name
of scolex.

The rings, or proglottides, also possess a peculiar
individuality, which is clearly shown in a considerable
number of species, as, after they have remained for

twelve successive phases of generation, but two only, one sexual
and the other non-sexual; the hydatids produced successively
from one another do not each represent a new phase of generation, but it is the echinococcus which represents this new phase ;
just as in plants, the succession of buds only represents the same
phase of generation.

Steenstrup, the author of the theory of *Alternate Generation,*
calls the non-sexual individual, which gives birth to the sexual
one, the *nurse ;* and he designates as *grand-nurse,* the non-sexual
one, which, when there are two non-sexual phases of development,
gives birth to the nurse. Van Beneden calls the nurse *scolex,*
and the grand-nurse *proscolex.*

Amongst the entozoa, the cestoid and trematode worms are
generally propagated by alternate generation; but the different
phases of their generation are accomplished in different situations. The animal cannot pass through the stages of larval
existence in the organ in which it becomes adult, and there is
consequently a necessity for migration into new organs and new
animals, this migration corresponding to each new phase of its
evolution.

some time continuously with each other, and with
the head or scolex, they become detached, and live
separately for a certain period. In several known
species of cestoid worms, the separation from the
scolex is effected before the rings have arrived at
maturity ; each ring lives, moves about, is nourished,
and increases in size in this free state, and its reproductive organs complete their development in the
same condition. This detached ring, which possesses
all the characteristics of animal life, is the adult
cestoid worm, which reproduces its species by means
of ova.

Before the ovum has been expelled from the
several organs, there is developed in it an embryo
which neither resembles the proglottis from which it
proceeds, nor the scolex which has produced the proglottis. It is, in fact, destitute of suckers, and armed
with six hooks which differ from those of the scolex
both in number and in form.

Here, then, are three successive and distinct
individualities, of which one forms the perfect animal.
How is the interrupted series between the embryo
and the scolex completed ? Does the latter come
from the former by metamorphosis, or by gemmation ?
Before proceeding further, the phases of alternate
generation in these successive individuals may be
recapitulated ; a ring is produced from the head by
gemmation ; and a six-hooked embryo is sexually
produced from the ring. The head is consequently a
nurse, according to the nomenclature of Steenstrup,
and a *scolex,* according to that of Van Beneden ; the
ring, or *proglottis,* is the adult individual.

No observer has traced in a decisive manner the

embryo during its transformation into the scolex; and we are therefore ignorant whether the latter is produced by metamorphosis or by gemmation, or whether there are not several generations interposed between the six-hooked vesicle and the scolex.

Some, as yet incomplete, observations lead to the idea that the embryo, when it has arrived at its *habitat*, loses its hooks, and is developed into a vesicle which produces the scolex by gemmation; in this case, the embryo would be a *grand-nurse* (Steenstrup), or a *proscolex* (Van Beneden). But, if the echinococcus be compared with the cœnurus, it will be understood that there is probably, in this respect, no uniformity of development amongst all the Tæniæ; and there are also probably many species which do not pass through a vesicular form.

The various phases of the development of a tœnioid worm are accomplished in different situations, as has been already observed. The adult individual, the proglottis, is developed and lives exclusively in the intestines; the ovum is always expelled from the intestines, and the embryo which it encloses must undoubtedly, before it becomes adapted to live in the intestines, pass into a new stage of development which brings it to the condition of a scolex, and which is accomplished in a different situation. The hooks with which the embryo is armed, and which are so arranged as to facilitate its movements through a resisting, and not through a fluid, medium, would support the supposition that this medium is a tissue, or a dense parenchymatous structure, and this supposition is, to a certain extent, confirmed by the fact of the constant absence of the larvæ of the cestoid

worms in either soft or hard water, and of the presence of a certain number of imperfect cestoid worms
in the parenchymatous organs, or in the closed
cavities, of animals.

Section A.   Tæniæ in the Larval Condition.   (Vesicular   Form.   Vesicular   or   Cystic   Worms).
   "Genera (?) Hydatis, and Echinococcus grouped
   together."   First Phase of Development; Hydatid
   (Acephalocyst).

This is generally a spherical, or oval, vesicle, of
very variable size, ranging from that of a pin's head
to that of the head of a fœtus at the full term of
gestation ; it encloses a limpid fluid ; it has thin
walls, which are not contractile, and are composed of
a homogeneous, elastic, fragile, transparent, whitish

Fig. 2.[1]

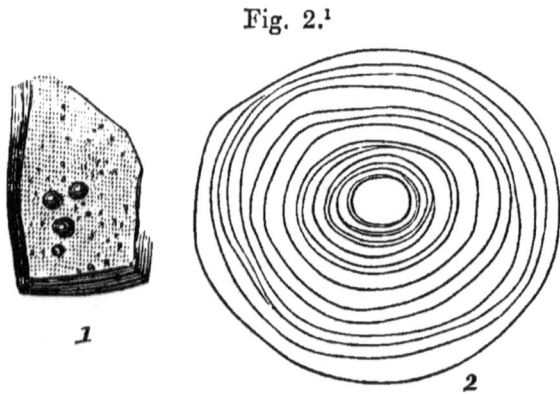

[1] Explanation of Figure 2.—Hydatid found in man.   1. A
fragment of the natural size ; at its edge are shown the layers of
which it is composed ; on the external surface are several hydatid
germs, of different periods of development.   2. One of the germs
flattened and magnified forty times ; it is formed, like the parent
hydatid, of stratified layers ; the germinal membrane is not yet
developed in its central cavity.

substance, similar in consistence to coagulated white of egg, not possessing any elementary granulations, fibres, or cells, and arranged in fine stratified layers, of extreme tenuity; it produces, by gemmation, either upon its external or internal surface, or in its substance, similar vesicles, which attain to a variable size, and in their turn reproduce others in a corresponding manner; the parent hydatid, and at a later period, the offspring, undergo considerable changes, lose their fluid, and become reduced to the state of flattened, dried-up membranes.

The hydatid vesicle, during its development, gives origin by its internal surface to a membrane (the *germinal membrane*), which forms an internal investment, and is composed of a fibrillary layer, infiltrated with elementary granules, and altogether different from the hydatid tissue. The germinal membrane is more or less apparent in certain parts of the hydatid vesicle; it adheres feebly to the wall of the vesicle, from which it is readily detached, when it dries up, and disappears some time before the hydatid. It is not found in all hydatids.

Second Phase of Development; Echinococcus.

The body of this entozoon is oblong or irregularly oval, scarcely visible to the naked eye, and divided into two parts by a circular contraction; the anterior part forms a head or scolex, furnished with a rostellum, which is armed with a double circlet of hooks, and with four contractile muscular suckers; numerous calcareous corpuscles are scattered about throughout its substance.

In the majority of instances the head is invagi-

nated in the caudal vesicle, and the echinococcus is
then regularly oval; the rostellum is also invaginated
amongst the suckers, like the retracted finger of a
glove, so that the hooks which most frequently have
their claws directed backwards are to be found
behind the suckers.

Fig. 3.[1]

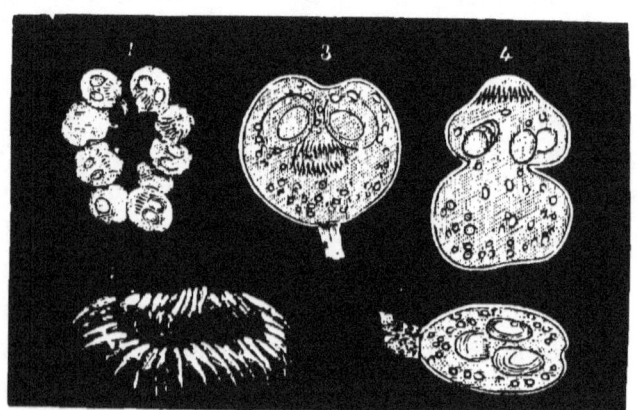

The echinococci are developed in the substance of
the germinal membrane, or rather in its expansions;
several of them spring up together and are connected
with the membrane by means of a little cord
(*funiculus*), which is inserted into a depression on

[1] Explanation of Figure 3.—Echinococci observed in man.
1. A group of echinococci, still adherent to the germinal membrane by means of funiculi; magnified forty times.   2. An echinococcus magnified 107 times; the head is invaginated into the
interior of the caudal vesicle; the funiculus is attached inferiorily.
3. The same, flattened; the head is retracted, and the suckers,
hooks, and calcareous corpuscles are shown.   4. An echinococcus
magnified 107 times; the head is protruded from the caudal
vesicle.   5. The circlet of hooks, magnified 350 times.

the caudal vesicle ; when the echinococcus has reached its full development, this cord breaks or becomes detached, and the echinococcus remains free in the cavity of the hydatid. After a certain period the germinal membrane is destroyed, and at a later period the echinococci are themselves lost, so that nothing then remains in the hydatid cavity excepting the hooks of the echinococci. Those hydatids in which no germinal membrane is developed have no echinococci.

The existence in the echinococcus of a rostellum, of a double circlet of hooks, of four suckers, and of calcareous corpuscles, indubitably place this parasite in the class Cestoidea, and in the sub-class Tæniæ. Considered by itself, that is to say separately from the hydatid, it represents a cystic worm, of which the body has not been developed, and which is consequently limited to a head and to a caudal vesicle.

Primitive and Ultimate Phases of Development of the Hydatid-Echinococcus.—The hydatid and the echinococcus being two successive and transitional phases in the development of a tænia, the six-hooked embryo of the tænia ought to precede the hydatid ; but whether the latter proceeds from the embryo by metamorphosis, or by gemmation, is not yet known.

The phase Scolex being always the last but one in the life of a cestoid worm, the echinococcus, which is a head or scolex, can produce nothing besides a proglottis, which is the adult cestoid worm, and forms the last link in the series. The various phases of the development of the tape-worm, which may be named the *Tænia Hydatigena*, are consequently four, at least, viz. :—

1. The Six-hooked Embryo ;
2. The Hydatid ;
3. The Echinococcus ;
4. The Proglottis.

According to the nomenclature of Van Beneden the second phase would be called the *Proscolex*, and the third (and penultimate) phase the *Scolex;* the more homely nomenclature of Steenstrup would furnish the designation of *Grand-nurse* for the hydatid, and of *Nurse* for the echinococcus.

Certain experiments, which consisted in causing dogs to swallow a large number of echinococci, have been made by Von Siebold, and repeated by Van Beneden, and their observations have led these distinguished writers to conclude that the echinococcus becomes developed into a perfect tænia in the intestinal canal of the dog.

Hydatids are not developed in a cavity invested with a mucous membrane, but in serous cavities, or in the substance of various organs ; and, in the latter case, they are always enclosed in an adventitious cyst.

Hydatids have been observed in man, in the ox, in the sheep, in the pig, in the monkey, and other animals which feed usually upon vegetables. They are almost, if not always, absent in carnivorous and in rodent animals, in birds, reptiles, and fishes.

The *hydatid-echinococci* probably form several species, but the points of difference which have been observed, either in the hydatids found in man and in animals, or in their echinococci, are not sufficiently great nor sufficiently precise to constitute distinct specific characters.

The presence or the absence of echinococci in an hydatid do not indicate any difference in the nature or in the species of that vesicle, for it is not an uncommon occurrence to find in the same cyst hydatids, which are exactly alike as regards their appearance, some of which contain echinococci, whilst the others do not.

Rudolphi has distinguished three species of echinococci,—*E. hominis, E. simiæ,* and *E. veterinorum,* but this distinction has been founded more upon the *habitat* of the worm than upon its zoological characters. Dujardin only describes the *E. veterinorum,* and Diesing places all the echinococci in one species, *E. polymorphus.* Küchenmeister divides them into two species,—the *E. veterinorum,* which he calls *E. scolicipariens,* and the *E. hominis,* which he calls *E. altricipariens;* this distinction appears to be founded more upon theoretical views than upon precise points of difference between the two species.

Genus (?) *Cysticercus.*—This is a solitary cestoid worm, provided with a voluminous caudal vesicle, with a head which possesses a double circlet of hooks and four suckers, with a neck, and with a more or less developed body, which is subcylindrical or flattened and marked by transverse furrows.

The body of the cysticercus presents deep furrows, but not segments completely separated like those of the tænia; it incloses a large number of calcareous corpuscles, but none are found usually in the caudal vesicle; the caudal vesicle is endowed with well-marked contractility, which it probably loses when it has grown old. In the majority of the cysticerci the head and the body are retracted and

c

invaginated in the caudal vesicle, which is then generally destitute of any external appendage, and presents at one point of its surface a slightly perceptible foramen.

As the cysticercus gets older it undergoes considerable changes ; a black pigmentary deposit invades the suckers, and especially the rostellum, which becomes of a firm consistence ; the hooks fall off, or are destroyed ; the foramen of the vesicle is contracted or entirely closed, and no longer permits of the extrusion of the head ; besides these changes, the vesicle becomes altered in form, and acquires an abnormal size, or is divided into segments, but it does not produce any new heads.

Cysticerci exist in serous cavities, and in parenchymatous organs ; in the latter case they are always enclosed in a cyst.   These worms are peculiar to the mammiferæ.

Cysticercus Cellulosæ[1] (Rudolphi).—This is an elliptic vesicle, upon which no external appendage is usually seen, provided with a very small and scarcely visible foramen ; the head is almost quadrangular ; this parasite possesses a double circlet of hooks, amounting to 32 in the cysticercus observed in man ; the neck is very short, and larger in front than behind ; the body is cylindrical, and longer than the vesicle ; the large diameter of the vesicle is about one-third of an inch.   The longitudinal furrows upon the head are strongly marked ; calcareous corpuscles

---

[1] The word *telæ*, with which the adjective *cellulosæ* agrees, is understood.   Its name is derived from its being found in the cellular, now called areolar, tissue.

are numerously disseminated throughout the structure of the worm.

Species or Varieties recognised by different authors.

Variety A. Cysticercus Fischerianus (Laennec). —Caudal vesicle pyriform; body attached to the large end of the vesicle; body and vesicle smaller than in the cysticercus cellulosæ. It has been found, as well as the following variety, in the human choroid plexuses.

Variety B. Tænia Albo-punctata (Treutler).— The vesicle is covered in some parts with a whitish substance, and possesses a sucker, and six hooks.

Variety C. Cysticercus Dicystus (Laennec).— This consists of two vesicles of unequal size, a single body, nearly an inch long, and a large-sized head; the suckers form four very black spots, visible to the naked eye; the hooks are enveloped in a mass of black matter. This worm has been found in the interior of the human cranium.

Variety E. Trachelocampylus (Frédault).—This is a cysticercus of a modified appearance, with the body retracted into the caudal vesicle. It has been observed in the human brain.

When the great changes, which take place in the cysticerci as they grow older, are considered, it is evident that the different species or varieties which have been described are only cysticerci in which considerable alteration in size or in appearance had occurred.

Most helminthologists admit that the cysticercus cellulosæ forms the scolex of the tænia soluim. It exists chiefly in the muscles, in the brain, and in the eye.   It has been observed in man, and in several mammiferæ.

Section B.   Tæniæ in the Perfect State.   (Ribbon-shaped form, or Free Proglottis).

The tæniæ, when in the perfect state, present themselves in two conditions.

1. In one the proglottis, shortly after being formed, leaves the scolex or the strobile before it becomes completely adult ; it lives free in the intes-tine, moves about, is nourished, increases and attains its perfect development as well as that which remains indefinitely adherent.

2. In another condition, which is perhaps the more common, the *Proglottides*, continuous with each other and with the *Scolex*, form a chain of varying length (the *Strobile*).   In this situation the *Proglot-tides* attain their complete development; those which are nearest to the scolex do not present any trace of reproductive organs, until the more distant ones, which are completely adult, present perfectly deve-loped ovules ; the male organ disappears first, and at a later period the female organ, in consequence of the rupture of the walls of the ovary, and sometimes, indeed, the proglottis, whose existence is terminated, still adheres to the common chain.

The ripe ovules always enclose a six-hooked embryo.   They exist in a prodigious number : Dujardin has calculated that in a tænia serrata,[1] a cestoid worm, which does not acquire a very great length, there were 25,000,000 eggs.   The ovules possess great tenacity of life, and can remain for a

[1] Very common in the small intestines of the dog.

very long time (as yet undetermined) without losing their vitality; this is not the case with vesicular worms, which die very quickly, and often waste away at the end of a few days.

The embryo having a very different shape from that of the tænia, cannot produce this worm excepting by a metamorphosis or by a new non-sexual generation. It cannot now be doubted that the tænia is reproduced by *Alternate Generation,* and it is even certain that the life of a tænia comprises more than two phases of generation. These phases are, without doubt, more numerous in certain species than in others; the *tænia hydatigena,* or the *tænia echinococcus,* probably possess one more phase than the tænia which proceeds from a cysticercus.

The vesicular condition ought to be regarded as one of the larval phases through which a tænia passes before arriving at the perfect state; but, has each adult tænia previously been a vesicular worm? We may reply with certainty, No; for, in fact, there are not less than two hundred species of perfect tæniæ, and there are scarcely more than twenty species of cystic worms. Besides this, the tæniæ of herbivorous animals cannot have been taken into the intestines in the vesicular form. The primitive phases of the development of the greater proportion of the tæniæ, are as yet entirely unknown. With respect to the adult tæniæ, whose vesicular form is supposed to have been decided, they are still small in number.

In order to arrive at this decision, we judge, partly, by the similitude of the head of a certain vesicular worm to that of a certain tænia; for instance, that of the *cysticercus fasciolaris* of the rat

to that of the *tænia crassicollis* of the cat; or
again, that of the *cysticercus cellulosæ* to that of
the *tænia solium*; and partly, by experiments which
have consisted in causing animals to swallow the
vesicular worms which, for some reason or other, are
supposed to be the larvæ of these tæniæ. These
experiments, which are deeply interesting, generally
offer, nevertheless, much room for error in the very
common existence of cestoid worms in the animals
which are experimented upon. The opposite experi-
ment which consists in making animals swallow the
ova of the tænia of another animal, with a view to
the production in them of vesicular worms, has been
also tried, and may, to some extent, serve as a means
of corroborating the results of the other form of
experimentation; but in these, as in the other experiments, it is scarcely possible to ascertain decisively
if the animals are not already affected by worms
similar to those which it is sought to communicate
to them.

Tænia found in Man (Tænia Solium).

Variety, or Species A. Tænia Armata.

In this worm the strobile is from 20 to 25 feet in
length, and, in some instances, the length may reach
to as many or even more yards; the strobile is
composed of perishable articulations, or rings (the
cucurbitini, or proglottides); the posterior rings are
quadrangular and oblong in shape, and increase in
length in proportion to their distance from the head;
the head (scolex) is furnished with four suckers, and
with two circlets of hooks.

The rings are frequently detached, and live for a certain period in a free state.

This worm exists in the human intestine, and very frequently only one exists in the same individual, from which circumstance the designation "Solium" was applied to it by Linnæus.

Fig. 4.[1]

Most writers admit that, according to the analogy between the form and arrangement of the heads of the tænia solium and of the cysticercus cellulosæ, and according to the experiments of Küchenmeister, Van Beneden, and others, the cysticercus cellulosæ is the larval state of the tænia solium.[2]

These experiments have been conducted in two ways : one by the ingestion of cysticerci into the

[1] Explanation of Figure 4.—The head of the *Tænia Armata*, magnified twelve times, and shown in two different positions. For the representation of the Tænia Solium Armata, see Fig. 13.

[2] It should be observed here that Dr. Davaine agrees with the minority that this point has not yet been settled beyond all doubts, owing to the small number of experiments which have been made, to their failure in some instances, and to the numerous sources of fallacy (already referred to) to which the experimenters were naturally exposed.

Other arguments in favour of the identity of the scolex of the cysticercus cellulosæ and that of the tænia solium, have been sought for in the frequency of this species of tænia in Abyssinia, where raw flesh is eaten, and at St. Petersburgh amongst those young children who are nourished with raw beef. But (as Dr. Davaine remarks) the flesh which is eaten in Abyssinia, as well as at St. Petersburgh, is beef and not pork, and it is only in the latter that cysticerci are observed, so that this argument falls to the ground, as it is based upon the supposition that the tænia solium is largely propagated through the employment, as an article of diet, of raw flesh containing cysticerci.

human stomach in order that they might be converted into the tænia solium, and the other by the introduction of the ova of this tænia into the stomach of the pig with a view to the development of the cysticercus cellulosæ in that animal.

Variety or Species B.   Tænia Inermis (Tænia mediocanellata, Küchenmeister).

This is a very long, broad, and thick tape-worm (much broader than the T. armata) ; its head, which is of a dark colour, and is not armed with hooks (whence its name), is large, and ·078 of an inch (2 millimètres) broad ; there is no rostellum, but the suckers are very large ; the neck is short, though more evident than that of T. armata ; the arrangement of the canals in the head is more simple than in the latter species of tænia, and the calcareous corpuscles are larger, and more numerous ; the posterior rings are very broad, being as much as ·66 of an inch (17 millimètres) in width, and from ·35 to ·54 of an inch (9 to 14 millimètres) in length ; the genital pores are irregularly alternate ; the proglottides are large, and very lively, sometimes issuing spontaneously from the anus between the periods of defæcation, and causing most unpleasant sensations ; when completely extended, the proglottides measure ·972 to 1·179 inches (25 to 30 millimètres) in length, and as much as ·273 of an inch (7 millimètres) in breadth ; the ova of the T. inermis are more oval, smoother, and clearer, than those of the T. armata, so that they allow of their embryos being more easily seen.

This tænia forms probably a distinct species, and not merely a variety of the T. solium.

Variety or Species C. Tænia of the Cape of Good Hope (Küchenmeister).

The scolex of this worm is unknown, the posterior part of the strobile having alone been observed ; its rings are thick and long, and are furnished, throughout the whole length of the body, with a longitudinal ridge ; the genital pores are marginal and alternate ; in some respects (the many-divisioned uterus and the ova) it is similar to the T. inermis.

Variety or Species D. Tænia of the Tropics. (Bothriocephalus Tropicus, Schmidtmüller).

This is a cestoid worm, whose characteristics have not yet been fully determined ; Schmidtmüller (quoted by Van Beneden) states that he observed it in one half of the negroes who were brought to the West Indies, and in some Europeans who had visited the coast of Guinea.

Tænia Nana (Bilharz).

This is a small cestoid worm, the whole length of which is only from about one-half to four-fifths of an inch (whence its name from the Latin *Nanus,* a dwarf); its body is filiform and flattened ; the head is broadest in front, and becomes gradually narrower towards the neck ; the suckers are of a sub-globular shape; the rostellum is pyriform, and armed with a circlet of bifid hooks ; the breadth of the rings is greater than their length.

This species of tænia has been found once by Bilharz, in a very considerable number, in the small intestines of a young man who had died of meningitis.

In accordance with the idea entertained by some helminthologists, that echinococci introduced into the human intestines may be developed into tæniæ, Küchenmeister suggests that the T. nana observed by Bilharz had a similar origin. The cases collected by Dr. Davaine appear, however, to point to a different conclusion ; out of thirty-six cases of hydatid tumours evacuated through the intestinal canal, not a single instance was noted in which tæniæ made their appearance ; in six of these an autopsy was performed, and no cestoid worm of any species was found in the intestines. To these cases might also be added those of hydatid tumours in communication with the bronchi, for in many of these cases the evacuation of the echinococci through the mouth occupied several months, and it is impossible that the patient could have avoided swallowing them in considerable quantity, both with the saliva and with the food ; yet in thirty-two such cases, collected by Dr. Davaine, not a single patient presented any signs of tæniæ, although a post-mortem examination was made in twelve of them.

Sub-Class II.—Bothriocephali.

These are cestoid worms, possessing a head or scolex, and rings furnished with male and female reproductive organs, the orifices of which open at the mid-line of one of the surfaces of each ring.

The Embryonic and the Larval conditions of these worms as are yet uncertain.

Genus Bothriocephalus (*Dibothrius*, Rudolphi).

The worms included in this genus have a soft, flattened, and elongated body, which is composed of numerous rings ; the head is oblong, and marked with two lateral depressions, running longitudinally, but it is not armed with any hooks ; the proglottides remain united.

Fig. 5.[1]

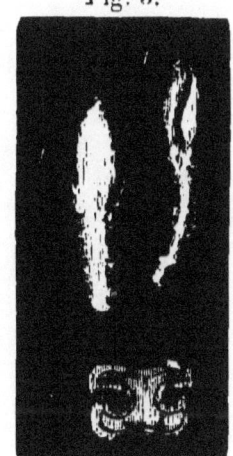

This genus comprises a large number of species, nearly all of which live in fishes ; the other species, which are few in number, and have been found in the mammiferæ and in birds, are but little known, with the exception of the species which exist in man.

The bothriocephali live in the intestinal canal.

The *Bothriocephalus latus* (found in man).

This worm is from twenty feet to as many yards in length, filiform in front, and sometimes an inch broad posteriorly ; it is usually of a deepish-red colour ; its head is oblong, and possesses two lateral elongated suckers ; the neck is almost wanting ; the first rings present a wrinkled appearance, those which come next are short and imperfectly square, and those which are situated still more posteriorly, measure more in the transverse, than in the longitudinal,

[1] Fig. 5, *i* and *h*.—Head of the Bothriocephalus latus, enlarged six times and seen in two different positions. *k*, transverse section of the head of the bothriocephalus found in the turbot, magnified twelve times ; this is introduced into the figure for the purpose of showing the arrangement of the lateral suckers.

direction; they present a thickening which is most marked near the centre of the ring, and they are sometimes perforated; the reproductive organs are situated about the median line.

Fig. 6.[1]

The bothriocephalus latus probably attains to a greater length than any other cestoid worm. Its rings do not become separated into cucurbitini like those of the Tænia solium, so that the posterior segments are often found still adherent to the strobile after the ova have been deposited; the discharge of the ova is usually effected by the rupture of the sides of the womb, and hence it frequently happens that the rings are perforated; sometimes the rings are divided longitudinally and constitute two laternal cords presenting a tail-like appearance, and at other times they are shrivelled up. As the bothriocephalus does not give off any cucurbitini, it breaks up into pieces which are almost always of considerable size, and which are only discharged from the intestines at distant intervals.

[1] Description of Figure 6.—The bothriocephalus latus, of the natural size, the fragments being taken at certain distances; the order of the letters indicates their relative situation, from the head to the posterior extremity; in c, d, e, f, the genital pore is visible; g, some of the terminal rings shrivelled up, after the deposition of the ova.

The head of the bothriocephalus assumes different forms, owing to the great contractility with which it is endowed, but it is always readily distinguishable from that of the tænia. The rings, when separated from the head, may also be very easily distinguished from those of the tænia, by the absence of a genital pore at the border, by the dark-coloured central thickening which has given rise to the comparison of the chain of rings of the bothriocephalus to the spinal column, and by the other characteristics of the tænia which have been already given.

The fecundity of the bothriocephalus, like that of the cestoid worms generally, is enormous. Eschricht has counted, in a single specimen, ten thousand rings, and reckoning at the rate of a thousand eggs for each ring, which is below the average, this would amount to ten millions of eggs from one bothriocephalus alone.

The ovum of the bothriocephalus is of large size; Dr. Davaine states that he has never been able to discover an embryo within it, but that, according to a drawing made by Schubart, of Utrecht, the embryo is ciliated, and armed with six hooks.

The bothriocephalus latus exists in the small intestines in man.

CHAPTER III.

TREMATODA.

THESE are solitary, non-articulated animals, more or less elongated and flattened ; they are provided with one or several organs of adherence, or suckers, with a soft integument not covered with vibratile cilia, with a mouth, and with an intestine, which is usually bifurcate, sometimes simple, sometimes ramifying, and which always has a cœcal termination ; they possess a nervous system, which is formed by a central mass and two lateral cords, and also a system of excretory canals ; they do not possess any circulatory apparatus ; they are generally hermaphrodite.

The trematode worms present two secondary types, which are completely distinct both as regards their organization, their mode of development, and their kind of life.

The first is that of the Polystoma (the Trematoda monogenesia of Van Beneden), and comprises those trematode worms which are furnished with more than two suckers. They have a direct development ; the embryo, which is unprovided with cilia at the moment of its being hatched, already possesses the form of the adult. All of them live as external parasites, upon the integument or the gills of aquatic animals, chiefly fishes ; they are never enclosed in a cyst.

It is unnecessary to give any further description of this type, as it has not been observed in Man.

The second type is that of the Distoma (the Trematoda digenesia of Van Benden), and comprises all the trematode worms which have not more than two suckers. Their development is indirect, the embryo bearing no resemblance to the parasite which has produced it. All of them, at the adult period, live in the interior of vertebrated animals.

The distoma never attain to a very large size; they are usually flat, and present a foliaceous appearance.

Their movements are very limited, and are principally accomplished by means of their suckers, similarly to the movements of leeches. Most frequently one of the suckers is situated at the anterior extremity, and constitutes at the same time the mouth; the other which is imperforate, and simply serves to fix the animal in position, is situated on the ventral surface, at some distance from the anterior sucker, or even at the caudal extremity; it is not found in every species.

With the exception of two species, all the distoma are hermaphrodite.

The ovum is sometimes completely developed within the oviduct. The embryo which it encloses is commonly furnished with vibratile cilia, and is occasionally armed with hooks; as has been already stated, it always differs greatly in its form and organisation from the individual which has given birth to it.

It is by *alternate generation* that the type of the individual which has produced the embryo re-appears; this latter, similar to an infusorial worm, has no distinct internal organs; it is generally covered with

vibratile cilia, by means of which it swims in surrounding fluids; it does not usually undergo metamorphosis, but it perishes after having produced
one or more germs, which are developed in its
interior. These germs enjoy a separate existence,
and continue to develop themselves; their organisation differs from that of the embryo which produced
them, and also from that of a perfect distomum.
They often become simple oval or cylindrical sacs,
each provided with a rudimentary sucker, or with
ramifying tubes without any apparent internal
organs; at other times they acquire a digestive tube,
and a buccal sucker.

These organisms, which proceed from the embryo,
form a second phase of generation. The embryo, after
being hatched, lived in a free state, but the individual
which succeeds it always lives parasitically in the
interior of molluscous animals. The individuals composing this second generation have been designated
sporocysts. They sometimes multiply themselves in
the same form, like the hydatids, either by division,
or by external or internal gemmation. The sporocysts are not destined to become perfect distoma;
they are endowed, in the early periods of their existence, with life and very active movements, and there
are subsequently formed in their interior germs which
increase rapidly; these germs by their accumulation
distend the body of the sporocyst, which, gradually
losing its vitality and its movements, is at length
reduced to the condition of a totally inert and membranous sac.

The germs developed in the sporocyst constitute
a third phase of generation which will produce the

perfect distomum ; at first, they form individuals to which the name of *cercariæ* has been given, and which are unlike the adult parasites ; their bodies are oval, very contractile, usually provided with temporary organs, such as a tail of variable length, which serves for locomotion, one or more hooks, which serve to penetrate into tissues, and with permanent organs, viz., suckers, a digestive tube, and an excretory apparatus. When the cercariæ have acquired a certain degree of development within the sporocyst, the latter is ruptured, and places its progeny in a state of freedom. The cercaria, having become free, swims in search of a new animal in which to live ; by the aid of its buccal hooks it penetrates through the integuments of some aquatic animal, usually the larva of an insect, or some mollusc, loses its tail in its passage, and becomes enveloped in a cyst ; in this new situation, it assumes the form of a perfect distomum, but it is only when the animal in which it is contained is swallowed accidentally by a vertebrated animal that the young distomum, having arrived into the organ and the animal which is suitable for its existence, permanently acquires the characteristics of the adult of its species.

Thus, the different phases in the development of a distomum are three in number : the embryo is a *grand-nurse*, the sporocyst is a *nurse*, and the cercaria is a *larva which arrives at the adult state by metamorphosis.*

The adult distoma never live in a free state ; and when they are removed from the organs which they inhabit and are placed in water, they rapidly become decomposed and perish. They are principally

D

found in the digestive tube, in the respiratory cavities, and in the biliary passages of vertebrated animals. They are more frequently found in aquatic animals or those which live in the vicinity of water than in animals which live in dry places; as may be observed in the amphibia amongst reptiles, in the wading and web-footed genera amongst birds, and in fishes amongst the vertebrata.

The distoma do not appear to be limited to certain parts of the globe, and they are also less exclusively peculiar to certain animals than is the case with other entozoa.

The distoma present four different forms which are distinguished by the number and by the position of the suckers, and which constitute four genera. Two of these are characterised by the existence of a single sucker, and are the monostomum and amphistomum of Rudolphi. In the monostomum the sucker is situated at the anterior extremity, in the amphistomum at the posterior extremity. The two other genera, the distomum and the holostomum, have an anterior buccal sucker and an abdominal sucker.

Genus Monostomum.

This genus comprises several species which are found in the intestines or other organs of birds, reptiles, and fishes.

The only species which has been observed in man is the *Monostomum lentis*, a very minute parasite found by Nordmann, in the lens of a patient who was affected with cataract.

Genus Distomum.

In the worms composing this genus the body is flattened or cylindrical, sometimes armed with hooks, and furnished with two distinct isolated suckers; of these, one is situated anteriorly and contains the mouth, whilst the posterior one is imperforate, and placed upon the ventral surface, near the mid-line, and at about one-sixth of the length of the worm from the anterior extremity; the intestine is divided into two branches, which are simple in some species, and ramified in others (as in the *Distomum hepaticum*).

This genus comprises a considerable number of species, all of which live parasitically, either in cavities which have a more or less direct external communication, or in closed cavities, or in cysts.

In the larval condition they exist in crustaceous and molluscous animals, or else in a state of freedom in the water; in the perfect condition, they are found in the animals belonging to the four classes of Vertebrata.

Distomum Hepaticum.

The body of this worm is of a whitish colour, and is from one-half of an inch to upwards of an inch in length, and from one-sixth to one-half of an inch in breadth, when full-grown; it is of an oval, oblong, or lanceolate shape, and is large and rounded in front, where it becomes suddenly contracted, so as to form a kind of conical neck; posteriorly it is narrow, and presents a leaf-like appearance; the integument is covered with flattened spines; the anterior sucker is terminal, and circular; the posterior

sucker is situated at a triangular orifice, very near
to the other ; a ramified intestine is distributed
throughout the entire body,
although it sometimes appears
to be absent in parts, owing to
its contractibility.   The embryo
of this species is unknown.

Fig. 7.[1]

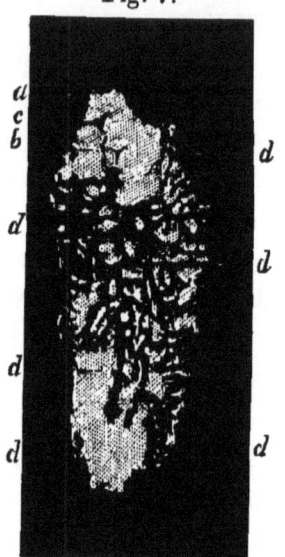

The distomum hepaticum
belongs especially to ruminant
animals, in which it is most
frequently found, but it is one
of the very limited number of
species of worms which can live
in animals of very different
nature.   It has been observed
in man, and in numerous domestic and wild animals.

It usually inhabits the gall-bladder and the biliary
passages, but it is not entirely confined to those
parts ; it has been met with in the intestines, and it
has also been seen in the blood-vessels in man, and
even in inflammatory tumours situated beneath the
skin ; it is probable that it never arrives at the adult
state in the latter situations.

Distomum Lanceolatum.

This parasite, which attains to about one-third
only of the dimensions of the distomum hepaticum,

---

[1] Fig. 7.—A distomum hepaticum, magnified.   *a*, the buccal
sucker ; *b*, the abdomidal sucker ;   *c*, the œsophagus ;   *d,d,d*, the
ramifications of the intestine ; they are not visible throughout
their whole length, in consequence of their contraction.

has been occasionally observed in man, but its usual *habitat* is in the biliary passages in the Ruminantia.

As is implied by its name, it is of a lanceolate shape, and it further differs from the D. hepaticum in the circumstance of the intestinal canal consisting of two straight, non-ramified divisions.

Distomum Heterophyes.

In this species the body is oblong, and flattened, smooth upon its under, and slightly convex upon its upper, surface ; the integument is covered by small spines, which are directed backwards ; the buccal sucker is small and funnel-shaped, and situated near the end of the body ; the ventral sucker is placed slightly in front of the middle of the body, and is of considerable size, being about twelve times larger than the buccal sucker.

This worm has been found, upon two occasions, by Bilharz, in the small intestines of children, where they were very numerous.

Distomum Hæmatobium.

In this species the two sexes are distinct, but the male, which is much larger than the female, contains the latter enclosed in a *canalis gynæcophorus*, so that the D. hæmatobium partakes, in some degree, of the hermaphroditic condition of the other species which constitute the genus Distomum.

It has, as yet, only been observed in Egypt. In man, it lives in the portal vein and its tributaries, and in the walls of the urinary bladder.

Distomum Ophthalmobium.

This is a very small trematode worm, of which species four specimens were observed by Gescheidt and Ammon in the eye of an infant affected with congenital cataract.

CHAPTER IV.

NEMATOIDEA.

THE worms included in this class have a long filiform, or fusiform, body, which is covered by a strong integument, composed of areolar tissue. The mouth is terminal, or nearly so; the intestine is straight, and runs throughout the whole length of the body; and the two sexes are separate.

The circulatory system is always rudimentary, even in those nematoidea which are most developed; and, although some writers have described a nervous system, its existence is very doubtful.

No respiratory apparatus has ever been ascertained to exist in any of these animals.

One or two longitudinal canals, which open upon the ventral surface not far from the mouth, most probably represent an excretory system. These canals are well-marked in the Anchylostomum duodenale, and in some of the Strongyli, and of the Ascarides.

The digestive apparatus is always very simple. The mouth differs in its conformation in the various genera of the Nematoidea, and it is often furnished with horn-like plates, or with actual hooks; the œsophagus, or the stomach, is also often dilated and muscular, or provided with horny plates, similar to those situated at the mouth; the remainder of the intestine is generally straight, and presents no special peculiarity.

The ova of the nematoid worms are round or elliptical, and sometimes burst whilst within the body of the mother, according to Dujardin.

The full-grown embryo possesses only the digestive tube, and the general envelop of the body; its mouth is not furnished with a complex apparatus, like that of the adult worm, and it has no reproductive organs.

It presents the general form of the adult, and attains to its complete development without undergoing any metamorphosis.

The female usually acquires much larger dimensions than the male, and it is also more frequently met with than the latter.

The Nematoidea form a very large number of species which, for the most part, live parasitically either in the hollow viscera, or in the tissues, of both vertebrate and invertebrate animals. The mode of transmission and of propagation of the nematoidea is only known in a small proportion of species. In some, the embryos are developed within the organ in which the parent worms are contained, and in which the latter had deposited their ova; in others, they are developed externally, and must, in order to attain to the perfect state, pass into their natural abode either in the condition of an embryo enclosed within the ovum, or else of a free larva. In the latter case, the larva sometimes possesses vital properties distinct from those of the adult, and it is able to resist the action of agents which would rapidly cause the destruction of the full-grown worm.

SECTION A.—NEMATOIDEA IN THE LARVAL STATE.

Nematoideum Tracheale.

This is a very minute larval nematoid worm, which has been only once observed by Mr. Rainey, who found several of the entozoa to which this name has been given, in the larynx and trachea of the body of a man.

These worms, which existed in a free state, exhibited great liveliness when they were first examined by the microscope; their movements gradually ceased, and some of the worms became rolled up in such a manner as to resemble a trichina when it is enclosed within its cyst; the others remained almost straight.

A full description of the Nematoideum tracheale is contained in the "Transactions of the Pathological Society for 1855."

SECTION B.—NEMATOIDEA IN THE PERFECT STATE.

Genus Oxyuris.

In the entozoa included in this genus the body is cylindrical, or almost fusiform, tapering off posteriorly in the female; the head is not armed with hooks; the mouth is round when it is contracted, triangular and three-lipped when it is projected.

The male oxyuris is very small, and is usually much rarer than the female.

The species which is found in man is the *Oxyuris Vermicularis*, which exists in the lower part of the large intestines, and especially in the rectum.

This entozoon is of a whitish colour ; its head presents two lateral wing-like expansions of the integument.

The male is only about one-third of the size of the female ; its tail is twisted spirally, the extremity of it forming a kind of sucker.

Fig. 8.[1]

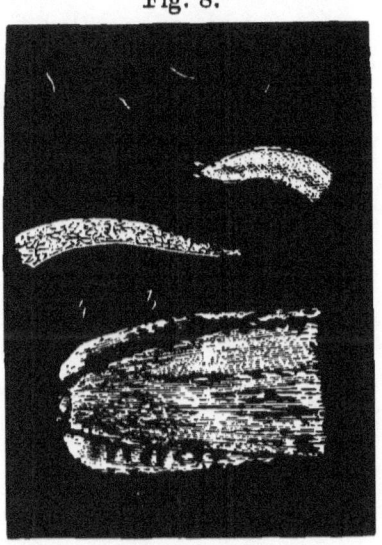

Genus Ascaris.

The ascarides are usually of a white or yellowish colour, and of a cylindrical form, thinner in some parts than in others ; their bodies are marked by four longitudinal opaque lines, which are placed opposite to each other ; the integument is striated tranversely ; the head is furnished with three distinct convex, semi-globular, valves, very similar to each other in appearance, of which one is placed

[1] Figure 8.—Female Oxyuris Vermicularis.—1. Four oxyurides of the natural size.—2. The cephalic end magnified ; the œsophagus and stomach are shown.—3. The caudal extremity magnified.—4. The head greatly enlarged ; *a*, the mouth furnished with three lips ; *b b*, the lateral expansions of the integument.

superiorly, and the others laterally and inferiorly; the valves, between which the mouth is situated, are marked on their internal surface with minute indentations.

The male is smaller than the female ; its tail is bent or twisted, and is sometimes provided with two lateral membraneous wings, or with two rows of papillæ, or more rarely with a sucker.

The genus Ascaris comprises many species which are found in the intestines of vertebrated animals.

The species which is often observed in the human subject is the *Ascaris Lumbricoides*. It varies from a few inches to a foot in length, and is very similar in appearance to the common earth-worm, for which it was formerly mistaken. The head of this entozoon is not armed with hooks, and the mouth is small,

Fig. 9.[1]

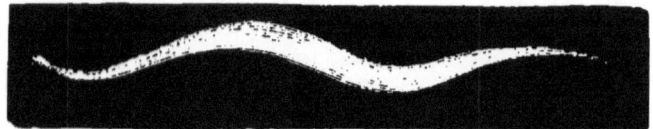

and furnished with three valves, which are minutely denticulated upon their inner surface ; the body is diminished in size towards either extremity, and it is striated transversely.

The ova of the Ascaris lumbricoides are not developed in the intestines, but are always expelled with the evacuations. Their development occupies a long period, and they pass through the autumn and the winter without any change taking place in them ; sometimes they may continue for even a year

[1] The Ascaris lumbricoides ; the worm in the figure is reduced to about one-third of the usual size.

in a state of inertia. The embryo remains enclosed within the shell, from which it never issues spontaneously; it lives there for more than a year, so that in those cases in which the ovum is slowly developed, more than two years may elapse between the formation of the ovum and the termination of embryonic existence.

According to Dr. Davaine's experiments, made upon dogs, it appears that the embryo remains shut up in the shell until the ovum is brought again into the intestines, and that, when it has arrived at this situation, the action of the intestinal juices soften the shell, which is pierced by the embryo, so that the latter is finally liberated.

The Ascaris lumbricoides lives in the small intestines.

Ascaris Alata (Bellingham).

The female of this species is about three and a half inches in length; its anterior extremity is bent, and furnished with two semi-transparent winglike expansions (whence the name), about one-tenth of an inch long; the tail is conical, and marked by a black spot.

Two females of this species have been observed on one occasion only by Bellingham, of Dublin, who states that he believes that the same species had been previously observed by Dr. J. V. Thompson. According to Dujardin, these entozoa are very similar to the ascaris of the cat, Ascaris mystax.[1]

[1] In an interesting paper contained in the "Lancet" of Jan. 10, 1863, Dr. Cobbold supports this view, and shows that the A. alata is more common in the human subject than it is generally supposed to be.

Genus Spiroptera.

The spiropteræ, which derive their name from the spiral tail of the male furnished with membranous, or vesicular, expansions, are found in vertebrated animals, and principally in the mammiferæ and in birds.

They often live between the coats of the stomach, or else in tumours situated in this organ, or in the œsophagus ; they are rarely found in other regions ; a very small number exist in a free state in the cavity of the intestine.

The only species which has been observed in the human subject is the *Spiroptera hominis*, which is stated by Mr. Lawrence to have been present in the urine of a female who passed a considerable number of these entozoa.[1] This species is doubtful.

Genus Trichina. (Owen).

This is a genus formed by Professor Owen, in order to include a small nematoid worm, the Trichina Spiralis, which is found, enclosed within a cyst, in the striated muscles.

It is a very minute cylindrical worm, coiled up into two, or two and a half spiral turns ; when it is unrolled, it measures about $\frac{1}{30}$th of an inch in length, and $\frac{1}{700}$th of an inch in diameter. The long axis of the cyst, within which the trichina is contained, lays between, and parallel to, the fibres of the muscle.[2]

---

[1] This case is recorded in the "Medico-Chirurgical Transactions," for 1812.

[2] For a representation of this entozoon, see Fig. 14.

Genus *Tricocephalus.*

In the worms which constitute this genus the body is very long, and is composed of two portions ; of these, the anterior portion is filiform, very narrow in front, and longer than the posterior portion, which is proportionately much broader, and which contains the reproductive organs and the whole of the intestinal tube with the exception of the œsophagus.

The Tricocephali are found in the cœcum, or some other part of the large intestines of man, and of the mammiferæ.

The species which is found in man is the

Tricocephalus Dispar.

In this entozoon the integument is striated transversely, with the exception of a longitudinal band which is thickly studded with minute papillæ ; the neck is very long, and like a fine hair in appearance. The posterior

Fig. 10.[1]

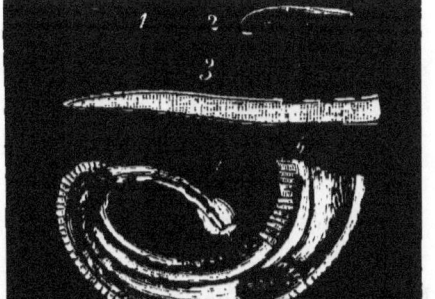

part is rolled up in the male, which is much smaller than the female, in which the posterior part is usually enlarged, and straight.

[1] Figure 10. The Tricocephalus dispar.—1. The male, of the natural size.—2. The female of the natural size.—3. The head magnified.—4. The tail also greatly enlarged.

The ova of the Tricocephalus are expelled with the evacuations, after they have been deposited in the intestine; but are not developed until some months subsequently. The embryo lives, for a considerable period, enclosed within the shell, and is not liberated until the ovum has re-entered the intestinal canal, through the medium of the food or of the drink.

The development of the Tricocephalus dispar, and the conditions attendant upon its propagation, closely resemble those of the Ascaris lumbricoides.

The Tricocephalus dispar exists in the cœcum; less frequently in the colon, or in the small intestines.

Genus Filaria.

The entozoa included in this genus are of either a white, yellow, or red colour, and of a soft consistence; they are cylindrical, and filiform in shape, and are very long, the length of the body being from 80 to 200 times greater than the breadth; the body usually tapers off slightly at one of its extremities; the head is continuous with the body, and is sometimes furnished with projecting papillæ, or with horn-like processes, which constitute a protection for it; the mouth is round or triangular; the integument of the body is smooth, or minutely striated in the tranverse direction.

The filariæ are found in vertebrated animals, principally in the mammiferæ and in birds, and more rarely in reptiles.

Three species, or varieties of filaria, have been observed in the human eye.

A. Filaria Lentis.

This has been found in the crystalline lens of the eye in persons affected with cataract.

B. Filaria of the Anterior Chamber.

A nematoid worm observed by Quadri in the aqueous humour of the anterior chamber of the eye.

C. Filaria of the Orbit.

This is a variety of nematoid worm which, according to Guyot, occurs beneath the conjunctiva of the negroes in Congo and the Gaboon.

Filaria Medinensis (The Guinea Worm).

This is a cylindrical thread-like worm, of a few inches in length, which sometimes, however, attains to the thickness of a quill, and may measure several feet. The male of this species is unknown. The female is of a whitish colour, and is marked by two longitudinal lines, situated upon opposite sides of the body ; the ova burst within its cavity.

This worm only exists in people living in Africa, India, or other hot counties, or who have recently left those parts. It lives in the subcutaneous areolar tissue of the limbs, of the body, and of the head.

Filaria Hominis Bronchialis

This is a nematoid worm, about one inch in length, which was observed by Treutler, who gave to it the name of *Hamularia Lymphatica*, in consequence of the two projecting hooks upon its under surface, and of the circumstance of its having been found in the bronchial glands.

Genus Anchylostomum.

Fig. 11.

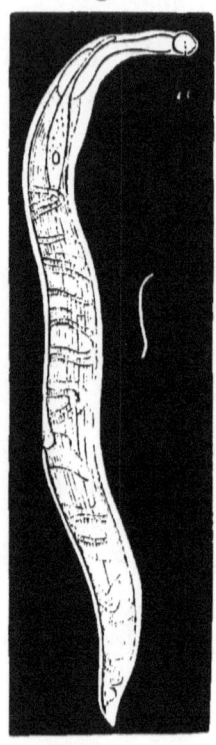

The anchylostomum is of an ashy colour, and cylindrical shape; the head is slightly tapering, and the mouth presents the appearance of a sucker, of horny texture, with a large circular opening; four teeth are situated within the inferior margin. The integument of the body is transversely striated.

This entozoon exists in man, and has been observed in Egypt, and also at Milan; the name which has been given to the species is *Anchylostoma duodenale*, its *habitat* being the duodenum, and the jejunum.

The female is more numerous than the male, and has been found in the proportion of 3 to 1 of the latter.

Genus Strongylus.

The strongylus is an entozoon of a cylindrical shape, which sometimes acquires a very large size, and reaches to several feet in length. The species

[1] Figure 11. Female Anchylostomum.—1. The worm of the natural size.—2. The same worm considerably enlarged.—*a*, The mouth.

which has been observed in man is the *Strongylus Gigas*, which is the largest of the nematoid worms.

It exists more frequently in the dog, the wolf, the horse, and some other animals. Its *habitat* is the kidney, and it has occasionally been found in the bladder, and in the sub-peritoneal areolar tissue, &c. Its colour, which is of a reddish tint, is probably due to the fluid in which it is immersed.

Only two or three strongyli usually exist in the same individual.

Strongylus Longevaginatus. (Diesing).

A small nematoid worm, of which several specimens were observed in the substance of the lung of a child six years old. The disease of which the child died is not recorded.

Genus Dactylius. (Curling).

In a case which came under the notice of Mr. Curling, in 1839, a young girl passed, upon several occasions, a considerable number of small worms with the urine. Some specimens of this entozoon, to which the name of *Dactylius Aculeatus* has been given, were examined by Mr. Curling, conjointly with Professors Owen and Quekett.

According to their description, this worm is of a light colour, cylindrical in form, and annulated, and tapering slightly towards either extremity. The female measures about four-fifths of an inch in length ; the male, as is the case with most nematoid worms, is much smaller, being only about two-fifths

E

of an inch long.   The head of the Dactylius is
obtuse, and truncated, and the mouth is orbicular.
The integument is armed with a number of sharp-
pointed spines, arranged in clusters of three or four,
and sometimes five, in longitudinal equidistant rows.

CHAPTER V.

ACANTHOTHECA.

THESE are solitary animals, having a complete digestive tube ; the mouth is situated
upon the inferior surface, and has a
pair of retractile hooks placed on
either side of it ; they have a distinct nervous system, and the sexes
are separate.

They present certain relations to
the Crustacea, and their embryos
bear an evident analogy to those of
the Lerneidæ, a species of crustacea
which lives parasitically in fishes.

Genus Pentastomum.

In the worms comprised in this
genus the body is oblong, cylindrical,
or flattened, and sometimes attains

Fig. 12.[1]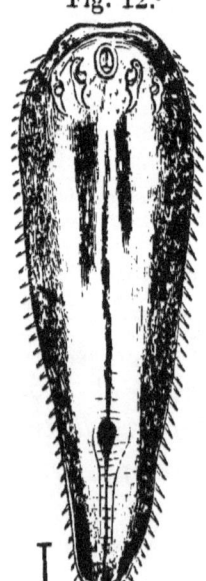

---

[1] Figure 12.   Pentastomum Denticulatum considerably enlarged.   A small line placed at the side shows the natural length
of this entozoon.

to the thickness of a goose-quill; it is much broader anteriorly than posteriorly; the two pairs of hooks, which are situated near the mouth, can be retracted into as many distinct cavities (whence this genus derives its name). The female is oviparous.

The Pentastoma live in the frontal sinuses, in the larynx, trachea, and lungs, or are contained in cysts upon the surface of organs.

These parasites have been observed in man, and in the mammiferæ, especially in reptiles. They seem to be more common in Brazil than in other parts of the world.

The two species which have been found in man are in the larval condition.

Pentastomum Constrictum.

This species has received its name from the transverse constrictions of its body, which, consequently presents an annulated appearance. The body is also rounded off anteriorly, and terminates posteriorly in a truncated cone; its integument possesses no spines.

This entozoon is about half an inch in length, and one-twelfth of an inch in breadth.

Pentastomum Denticulatum.

The body of this worm is of a white colour, and is larger in front than behind; it is convex upon its upper, and flattened upon its lower surface; it is also annulated, and is covered with a number of spines.

This entozoon is probably the larva of the *Pentas-*

tomum Tænioides, which is found in the dog and some other animals.

It has been frequently met with in the human subject of late years, by different observers at Vienna, Leipsig, and Dresden. In all of these cases, with only one exception, it was found enclosed within a small fibrous cryst, situated upon the surface of the liver ; in the single exception referred to, it existed upon the surface of the kidney.

It does not appear to create any special derangement in the functions of the organ in which it is contained, owing to its very minute size.

PART II.

THE PATHOLOGY AND TREATMENT OF HUMAN ENTOZOA.

CHAPTER I.

GENERAL REMARKS.

THE MANNER OF DISTRIBUTION OF THE ENTOZOA IN VARIOUS
PARTS OF THE BODY.—THE CONDITIONS WHICH INFLUENCE
THE EXISTENCE AND FREQUENCY OF ENTOZOA.—THE EFFECTS
OF GEOGRAPHICAL POSITION, OF CLIMATE, OF THE SEASONS,
OF MOISTURE, OF DIET, OF SEX, OF CONSTITUTION, AND OF
AGE, UPON THE PROPAGATION OF ENTOZOA.—THE SYMPTOMS
AND COMPLICATIONS CAUSED BY WORMS.

No part of the body, in vertebrated animals, is free
from the attacks of entozoa. The most inaccessible situations, such as the interior of the eye, the
brain, and the spinal canal, are sometimes affected
by these parasites; and even the medullary cavity
of bones has furnished instances of their invasion.

As a general rule, entozoa of the same species
are not found in different organs; the small intestine of man is the *habitat* of the ascaris lumbricoides, of the tænia solium, and of the bothriocephalus latus, but neither of these species is nor-
mally met with in the stomach or in the large
intestine. The principal viscera of the body are

affected by special worms ; for instance the cæcum is infested by the tricocephalus, the rectum by the oxyuris, the biliary passages by the distomum hepaticum, and the urinary organs by the strongylus gigas.

Like the viscera, the other parts of the body have their peculiar entozoa ; the trichina spiralis is found in the voluntary muscular tissue, the cœnurus is found in the central nervous system, and the cysticercus and the echinococcus are met with only in natural or adventitious serous cavities.

This limitation of certain worms to certain regions is observed with such regularity that it may be considered as the result of a general law.

The development and the propagation of entozoa are influenced by various conditions, which are sometimes external, such as the geographical position, the climate, and the seasons, and sometimes peculiar to the individual affected, such as the age and the sex.

Of all the influences which bear upon the existence of entozoa, that of geographical position is the most evident, and was even well-known to the ancients. This question may be considered from two points of view ; 1. That there exist in certain countries entozoa which are not observed elsewhere ; 2. That the number of persons affected by worms is much more considerable in some countries than in others.

The filaria medinensis is developed exclusively in tropical countries ; the anchylostomum duodenale has, as yet, only been observed in Italy (at Milan), and in Egypt ; the tænia nana and the distomum hæmatobium have never been met with excepting in the

latter country; and the existence of the bothriocephalus latus has been satisfactorily proved in
Europe only.

Some species of entozoa are, however, almost
universally diffused; these are the tœnia, the oxyuris,
and the ascaris lumbricoides.

With respect to the greater relative frequency of
certain species of worms in certain countries, that
of the tœnia in Egypt, and in Abyssinia, for example,
is generally acknowledged; that, again, of the
bothriocephalus in particular districts of Sweden, of
Russia, and of Switzerland; that of the ascaris
lumbricoides amongst the negroes, and also. that of
hydatid worms in Iceland.

The influence of locality upon the existence of
entozoa depends upon various conditions of which
the exact ratio is usually very uncertain; the climate
always appears to be the principal condition affecting
the existence of the filaria medinensis, and this is also
possibly the case with regard to the anchylostomum
duodenale and the distomum hæmatobium.

An influence which is less permanent, but which
is, in some respects, equal to that of climate, is produced by the seasons. These bring with them variations of temperature, of moisture, and of diet, which
favour the development or transmission of certain
species of worms, and which consequently render
these species more or less common, according to the
different periods of the year.

Amongst the conditions which are favourable to
the development of entozoa, and which are dependent
upon the climate or the season of the year, moisture
is one of the most apparent. Prolonged rains in

tropical countries may give rise to actual epidemics of the Guinea-worm ; amongst animals, the influence which a humid character of the pastures exercises upon the frequency of the distomum hepaticum in sheep is well known, and it is stated that, in India, the filariæ observed in the eye of the horse become much more common in the cold season, after the abundant rains.

A considerable relative degree of importance in the production of worms has been assigned to the manner of living. Sailors, for instance, are very rarely affected with hydatids ; Dr. Budd thinks that this exemption may be attributed to the circumstance that their diet, which consists chiefly of salt meat, is probably unfavourable to the development of cystic worms.

It is a generally received opinion that it is the mode of living which renders the oxyurides and lumbrici more common amongst children than amongst adults ; and this opinion seems to be confirmed by the fact that children residing in large towns are less frequently attacked by these species of entozoa than those who live in the country. Dr. Davaine states, however, that his own observations have led him to the conclusion that the greater relative frequency of intestinal worms in the country is due not to the use of fruits, of green leguminous plants, and of farinaceous substances as articles of diet, but to the quality of the water which is employed for drinking and for culinary purposes.

The common occurrence of the tænia in adults does not appear to depend so much upon a good or a bad diet, as was formerly supposed, but rather upon the ingestion into the stomach of insufficiently cooked meat.

Age is another of the conditions which are most evidently connected with the frequency or the rarity of entozoa. In the human subject, the various species of worms are unequally common at different periods of life, and are relatively rare amongst very young infants, and in old people.

Although several cases of entozoa in the fœtus have been recorded by the earlier writers, they are of a very doubtful character, and when we take into consideration the circumstance that most erroneous ideas at one time prevailed upon the subject of worms, it is probable that these authors were mistaken in their observations.

In infants at the breast worms have been more frequently observed, and numerous cases are known in which nematoid, trematode, and more often cestoid, entozoa of considerable size have been seen in children only a few months old. Some writers have brought this fact forward as an argument in support of the theory of spontaneous generation, or of that of hereditary transmission of worms ; but it appears rather to serve as an evidence of the rapid growth of certain species of entozoa, or of the influence exercised by various accidental causes.[1]

[1] The frequent occurrence of tape-worm amongst children, of from eight to twelve months of age, and still at the breast, who were brought under my notice at the Metropolitan Free Hospital, induced me to inquire into the reasons for this. In the majority of cases, I learnt that the mothers, actuated by an erroneous notion of strengthening the infants, or of sustaining them during the day-time whilst they themselves went out to work, were in the habit of occasionally giving the children pieces of raw meat to suck.

At about the age of two years entozoa become common; but the question of the frequency of worms, in relation to the age of the individuals affected by them can only be considered in a general manner. Certain entozoa are more frequent at a particular period of life, as is the case with the oxyuris and the ascaris lumbricoides, which are most usually met with in childhood, whilst other species are observable, in nearly equal proportion, at all ages.

Sex exercises a remarkable influence upon the frequency of tænia, and this singular fact has been remarked by many helminthologists, the cases of tænia occurring in females being as three to two, when compared with the cases occurring in males.

The constitution, or the actual state of the health, of an individual is commonly looked upon as one of the predisposing causes of the existence of worms; and, from the fact that certain epizoa (parasites affecting the external parts of the body) attack the integuments of diseased and badly nourished animals, it may be inferred that something analogous occurs with regard to the entozoa. The term *helminthiasis* is applied by some writers to this constitutional predisposition, when it is strongly marked.

CHAPTER II.

ENTOZOA FOUND IN THE RESPIRATORY PASSAGES.

THE respiratory passages in many animals furnish a *habitat* for certain species of worms, and numerous examples have been observed amongst mammiferæ, birds, and reptiles; but our present knowledge concerning the entozoa which exist in these situations in man is very limited.

The entozoon, described by Treutler as the Hamularia lymphatica, was found in the bronchial ganglia, and not in the air passages themselves; besides which the existence of this worm as a distinct species must be considered very doubtful.

Another entozoon, the Strongylus longevaginatus, which is supposed by some writers to be similar to the Hamularia lymphatica, has been once observed in a boy's lungs, from which several of these small nematoid worms were taken after death; some of the worms appeared to be imbedded in the lung-substance, whilst others existed in a free state in the ramifications of the bronchi.

Nematoid worms in the larval condition, which cannot consequently be referred to any known species, have been found in a state of freedom in the human larynx and trachea. These worms were still alive, and in such numbers that it cannot be supposed that they were only the result of an accidental migration from elsewhere.

These entozoa, of which an account has already been given, under the head of Nematoideum tracheale, in the Synopsis, were discovered by Mr. Rainey, during the examination of the body of a person who had died of an affection of the lower extremities.

The other entozoa which have been found in the larynx, the trachea, or the bronchi in Man, were not developed in those parts, but had been introduced from elsewhere, either through the upper opening of the larynx, or through a perforation of one of the branches of the bronchi.

The worms which may find their way through the superior aperture of the larynx are the ascarides lumbricoides, which have come from the intestinal canal; and those which may accidentally pass into the air-passages through a perforation of one of the bronchial branches, are hydatids, which have been previously developed in one of the viscera of the thorax or of the abdomen.

Little can be said of the treatment which should be adopted in these cases until our knowledge of the entozoa which occasionally affect the air-passages is more extended.

If the existence of any worms in the air-passages should be strongly suspected, or completely diagnosed, the most appropriate treatment will consist in the administration of expectorants, together with the inhalation of the vapour of assafœtida, of ether, of spirits of turpentine, of tar, or of tobacco, most of which plans have been found efficacious in the treatment of animals affected with entozoa in the respiratory passages.

CHAPTER III.

GENERAL REMARKS CONCERNING THE ENTOZOA WHICH AFFECT THE ALIMENTARY CANAL.

As might be supposed from the facility of external communication through the medium of the mouth and œsophagus, and from the fact of the entozoa being carried into the body, in the form of ova, along with various articles used as food, the intestinal canal is more subject to the invasions of these parasites than any other part of the body.

Generally speaking, only one species of intestinal worm occurs, in one individual, at the same time, but the existence of one species does not necessarily prevent that of another. Rosen reports the case of a child, four years old, who passed at the same time ten ascarides lumbricoides, a large number of oxyurides, and a considerable portion of a tænia. Facts similar to this are very rare; but cases in which two species of entozoa are present in the intestines are not uncommon.

Children are comparatively more subject to nematoid, and adults to cestoid, worms; and females suffer from intestinal entozoa more frequently than males do.

As a common rule, persons are only affected by these parasites during a limited period; although there are some individuals who are never entirely exempt from them.

The presence of worms in the intestines does not always give rise to marked symptoms, and may even be compatible with an apparently good state of health, but in a large proportion of cases some symptoms, of either a local or a sympathetic character, are evident.

The local symptoms consist chiefly in disturbance of the digestive functions, in abdominal pains, and in itching at the anus.

Most of the organs of the body may participate in the sympathetic disturbance produced by the existence of intestinal entozoa.

The imaginary perception of disagreeable odours, the dilatation of the pupil, the permanent or temporary impairment of vision, the morbidly exaggerated sense of hearing, the perversion of the taste, the itching and tingling of the skin,—any or all of which may occur,—show the sympathetic action upon the senses ; and, on the other hand, the drowsiness or giddiness, the disturbed dreams, the convulsive spasms, the wandering pains, the cough, the difficulty of breathing, the palpitation of the heart, the intermittent character of the pulse, the insatiable hunger or thirst, the salivation, and the emaciation, equally afford evidence of the effects which are produced upon the nervous system, the organs of respiration, of circulation, and of digestion, and upon the secretions and nutrition.

In countries where entozoa are comparatively rare, many of these phenomena may not be observed, or may arise only in a modified degree ; but, in those districts in which worms attack nearly the whole of the population, the most varied complications are attributable to the presence of these parasites in the intestines, and are constantly treated and cured by the administration of anthelmintics.

The absence or appearance of functional disorders, and their variable frequency or intensity, cannot be explained simply by the different nature of the intestinal worms ; the tænia, the bothriocephalus, the ascaris lumbricoides, and the oxyuris, although very dissimilar in their character, may give rise to almost similar symptoms. The number, and the size of these entozoa are doubtless not without some influence upon the pathological phenomena, and their presence in the stomach is usually attended with graver symptoms than are produced when they are in the intestines ; but, beyond this, the severity of the symptoms depends chiefly upon the constitutional condition, and the degree of nervous susceptibility of the individual who is affected,—females, as a rule, suffering more than males.

The following is a summary of the symptoms which have been remarked by different observers ; some of these are very common, and others have been only rarely observed.

The colour of the face is changed, sometimes flushed, sometimes pale, and sometimes of a leaden hue ; a bluish semicircle appears beneath the eyes, which are less brilliant ; the lower eyelids are swollen, the pupils are dilated, and the eyelids and conjunctivæ are sometimes of a yellowish hue ; the patient complains of an intolerable itching about the nostrils, occasional hemorrhage from the nose, and frequent and severe headache ; the mouth is full of saliva, and the breath is fetid ; there are grinding of the teeth, disturbed sleep, somnambulism, fainting, giddiness, and buzzing sounds in the ears; considerable thirst ; a dry, spasmodic cough ; difficulty of breath-

ing, hiccough, and impairment of the powers of
speech ; palpitation of the heart, and hard, frequent,
or intermittent pulse ; the abdomen is swollen, and
the patient complains of frequent, nauseous eructa-
tions, and griping pain ; the appetite is occasionally
lost, and at other times it is greatly augmented ;
there is a sensation of pricking and tearing which is
not fixed to one spot, but shifts about the whole
cavity of the abdomen, and which is increased when
the stomach is empty, and lessened after food has
been taken ; heart-burn, diarrhœa, or constipation
are present, and the urine is limpid ; the body
becomes emaciated ; violent itching or cramps are
felt in the neighbourhood of the anus ; there are
lassitude, anxious and restless manner, and sometimes more or less disturbance of the mental functions.

These phenomena occasionally become so severe
as to induce or to simulate epilepsy, tetanus, hysteria,
strabismus, amaurosis, paralysis, coma, or even
insanity. The best proof which can be given that
such affections may be caused by the presence of
intestinal entozoa, consists in the fact that they
disappear immediately after the expulsion of the
worms either accidentally or by the administration of
proper remedies.

None of these symptoms, taken singly, furnish a
decided indication of the existence of worms in the
intestines ; but the occurrence of several of them,
conjointly, in the same person, renders a thorough
investigation into the case necessary.

The expulsion from the bowels of some oxyurides,
or of a portion of tape-worm, or of an ascaris lumbricoides (of which species, however, only a single worm

sometimes exists) may be regarded as a pathognomonic sign of the presence of one of those species of worms in the intestinal canal; but some species of entozoa, and the ova of all the intestinal worms, can only be detected by means of a microscopic examination.

The affections produced by the existence of intestinal entozoa do not, in general, follow a regular course. They very often make their appearance suddenly, and are followed by remissions of variable length, and, frequently also, there is some predominant symptom of an unusual character, which comes on unexpectedly and goes away again without any apparent cause, and at no certain period; whilst the symptoms bear no relation to one another.

When the entozoa leave the intestines and pass into other organs, either through natural or accidentally-formed passages, they often give rise to new symptoms or complications.

The entozoa which are observed in the human intestines belong to the protozoa, and to the cestoid, trematode, and nematoid classes of worms. Several species have only been met with once, or upon very few occasions.

To the protozoa the following belong :—The vibrio, the cercomonas hominis, and the paramecium coli.

The cestoid intestinal worms are :—The tænia solium, the bothriocephalus latus, and the tænia nana.

The only trematode worm found in the intestines is the distomum heterophyes.

The nematoid intestinal worms are :—The anchylostomum duodenale, the ascaris lumbricoides, the ascaris alata, the tricocephalus dispar, and the oxyuris vermicularis.

F

The parts of the intestinal canal in which these entozoa live are as follows :—In the small intestines are found the vibrio, the cercomonas hominis, the tænia solium, the bothriocephalus latus, the tænia nana, the distomum heterophyes, the anchylostomum duodenale, the ascaris lumbricoides, and the ascaris alata ; the tricocephalus dispar inhabits the cæcum, and the paramecium coli and oxyuris vermicularis infest the large intestines.

No entozoa are found, excepting as an accidental circumstance, in that part of the alimentary tube which extends from the mouth to the pylorus.

Hydatids and the distomum hepaticum, which have wandered from their usual *habitat,* have also been met with in the intestines.

CHAPTER IV.

INTESTINAL PROTOZOA.

PROTOZOA, or infusoria, of different species, are developed in vegetable and animal substances which are undergoing putrefaction. It might be supposed that those which exist in the matters which are still contained within the intestines are developed in that situation as a result of putrefaction, but there is an important distinction between the infusorial worms which are developed in a free state, and those which are, properly speaking, intestinal protozoa. Those which exist in the fæcal matter, prior to its evacuation, perish as soon as the temperature, which has been acquired in the body, is lost ; and they cannot, consequently, be considered as identical with infusoria which are produced during the slow putrefaction of any substance, but rather as real parasites which find in the intestines the conditions necessary for their existence.

According to Dr. Davaine, who has paid much attention to this subject, intestinal protozoa are not ordinarily found in the evacuations of healthy individuals, but only in those of persons who suffer from some alvine flux such as occurs in cholera, in the diarrhœa of phthisical patients, and in dysentery.

The intestinal protozoa which have been described up to the present time (if we except some of those which have been observed by Leuwenhock, of which the nature has not been fully determined) belong to three distinct genera, viz., the vibriones, cercomonades, and paramecia.

To the genus vibrio may be referred the animalculæ, which have been remarked by Pouchet and others in the peculiar rice-water dejections of choleraic patients ; they have not hitherto been discovered in the analogous matter which is vomited.

Dr. Hassall believes that it is probable that these animalcules are introduced into the stomach and the intestines through the medium of the atmospheric air, or of the water which is used for drinking purposes, and that, finding conditions favourable to their existence, they are developed and multiplied with almost inconceivable rapidity.

Vibriones have been observed, although in very small number, in the evacuations of healthy persons, by both Dr. Hassall and Mr. Rainey. The circumstance that vibriones are widely diffused throughout nature, and that they are developed in all vegetable and animal infusions, at all seasons of the year, suffices, according to the former observer, to show that there is no essential connection between the existence of these parasites and the visitation of cholera ; but yet the invariable presence of these animalcules in considerable numbers in the dejections of choleraic patients constitutes an interesting fact, and it cannot be supposed that they are altogether without influence upon the appearance and aggravation of the symptoms.

The cercomonas hominis was invariably observed by Dr. Davaine in the fluid dejections of the patients suffering from cholera, who were admitted into the Charité Hospital at Paris, during the epidemic of cholera in 1853-54 ; so numerous, in fact, were these protozoa that each drop of fluid, when examined under the microscope, was found to contain several cermonades. Dr. Davaine was unable to determine whether there was any actual relation between the presence of these infusoria and that of cholera.

Animalcules very similar in their appearance to the cercomonades of cholera, but not quite identical with them, were noticed by the same physician in a case of typhoid fever.

The protozoa observed by Malmsten, of Stockholm, in some cases of cholera and diarrhœa were referred to the genus Paramecium, to which also probably belonged a species which was discovered by Leuwenhock.

Professor Malmsten considers that these animal-

cules, living, as they do, even in the mucus contained
between the villi of the intestine, endowed with
great motility and vivacity, and so numerous that
from 20 to 25 of them may be found in a single drop
of mucus, must by the irritation which they induce
increase the intestinal secretion and the peristaltic
action of the bowels.

Injections, acidulated with nitric acid, appeared
to him to be the only means of destroying the paramecia, and of checking the lienteric diarrhœa which
is caused by them. It is probable that the administration by the mouth of the dilute acids would fulfil
the same indication.

CHAPTER V.

THE CESTOID WORMS FOUND IN THE HUMAN INTESTINES.

OF the three kinds of cestoid intestinal worms, only
two, the tænia solium and the bothriocephalus latus,
need occupy our attention, as the third, the tænia
nana, has never been observed excepting in Egypt.

Although there is no complete incompatibility
between the two genera referred to above, they
usually exist in different countries, and appear almost
to exclude one another; for, generally speaking, in
any locality where one of these entozoa is common,
the other is not observed or, at any rate, only in very
rare cases.

The bothriocephalus is less widely spread than
the tænia, and is found in limited districts, which are

principally situated upon the borders of the sea, and of certain lakes, or rivers. It is well known only in Europe.

The tænia solium has been observed in Europe, in Asia, in Africa, and in America, and it probably exists all over the world. It has been stated by Schmidtmuller that the Malays do not suffer from cestoid worms, but the data upon which the assertion is founded are incomplete.

The tænia solium prevails in some countries of Europe to the exclusion of the bothriocephalus, viz., in England, France, Spain, Greece, Italy, Austria, and Prussia.

The bothriocephalus latus prevails to the almost entire exclusion of the tænia in Switzerland and in Russia; both entozoa are more or less common in Holland and in Sweden.

These general facts admit of some exceptions, either of a local or accidental character, and, in consequence of its being brought from another district, either of these worms may be observed in a district which it is not ordinarily found in.

The bothriocephalus is most common in Switzerland, and occurs so frequently at Geneva, that Dr. Odier, a distinguished medical practitioner in that city, states that nearly a fourth of the inhabitants are affected by it at some period or other during their lifetime. This entozoon is also very prevalent in those countries which are bounded by the Baltic Sea.

It has been observed that, with regard to the part of Europe which comprises Russia and Germany, the bothriocephalus is found only to the eastward of the Vistula, and that it is rare, whilst the tænia is comparatively common, in the districts situated upon the western side of that river. Some writers, Von Siebold amongst the number, go so far as to look upon the Vistula as a complete line of demarcation between the two genera, in the countries which constitute Western Europe.

Owing to the circumstance that the countries in which the bothriocephalus is endemic border upon the sea, lakes, or rivers, the cause of the existence and of the frequency of this worm has been naturally sought for in some condition which is common to these various countries.

It was for a long period supposed to depend upon the fish diet which is largely used by the inhabitants of these localities, but arguments, chiefly founded upon the limitations of the appearance of the bothriocephalus to certain districts, and to its total absence in others, where a fish diet is also much employed, have not been wanting to invalidate this view; and it is highly probable that if this be one of the causes, there are others of a local character which are equally active.

The existence of the bothriocephalus in particular countries which bear an evident analogy to each other, and that of tænia in countries of a most dissimilar nature,—situated at the sea-coast as well as in the centre of continents, in arid deserts, under all latitudes, and at various heights,—shows a marked distinction in the mode of propagation of these two cestoid worms.

There are good reasons for the belief that the transmission and propagation of the tænia solium

depend upon special circumstances connected with diet.
So long ago as 1804 it was remarked by Dr. Fortassin
that those persons who are occupied in the mani-
pulation of fresh animal matter are more frequently
affected with tape-worm than those who follow some
other trade ; and this opinion has since then been
supported by most writers on the subject.

Out of more than two hundred patients under
the care of Wawruch, one-fourth followed the calling
of a cook ; and it is stated that, in India, the members of a particular caste, who employ an almost
exclusive vegetable diet, are not attacked by tænia,
which is nevertheless common amongst the other
natives.

Of themselves, these observations have no great
importance, but they are interesting when considered
together with the following facts.

The tænia solium, as is well known, is extremely
frequent in Abyssinia, and nearly all the inhabitants
of that country are affected by it.   Various reasons
have been given in order to account for the frequency of this malady ; some travellers have attributed it to the quality of the water, and others to a
kind of grain, called Teff, from which the native
bread is made, but the majority (including our countryman, James Bruce,) have stated their belief that
it is due to the use of raw meat as an article of food.

In Russia, where the bothriocephalus ordinarily
prevails to the exclusion of the tænia solium, a
curious circumstance occurred some few years since.
In order to check the ravages of an epidemic of
dysentery, which was generally fatal amongst very
young children, in St. Petersburgh, the expedient

was resorted to of nourishing the little patients with raw beef. Most of the children who were subjected to this mode of alimentation recovered; but it was soon ascertained that several of them had become affected with tænia.

From the preceding accounts it will be seen that in a country where the tænia is common, those persons who abstain from raw meat are alone free from the attacks of that entozoon; whilst in another country, where tænia was scarcely known previously, those only who eat uncooked flesh were affected by this worm, and this latter result occurred in young children in whom the tænia solium is always more rare than in adults.

It has been advanced by many writers that the cysticercus found in the cellular tissue is converted into the tænia solium in the human intestine, but, as Dr. Davaine observes, the cysticercus is not found in beef although it is very common in pork.

Hence Dr. Davaine further remarks, that it must be concluded that if beef which does not contain the cysticercus propagates the tænia, and if this worm is sometimes present in persons who do not eat pork (the Jews, for instance),[1] the cysticercus cellulosæ is not the scolex, or head of the tænia solium, or else that, at least, the tænia possesses some other mode of propagation.

[1] Cases of tænia are more frequent amongst the Jews than is usually supposed. At the Metropolitan Free Hospital, which is situated near Hounsditch and other parts of London inhabited by members of this persuasion, and where a large number of the poorer Jews apply for medical relief, I have frequently had opportunities of verifying this fact.

CHAPTER VI.

THE TÆNIA SOLIUM.

THE small intestine is the ordinary habitat of the

Fig. 13.[1]

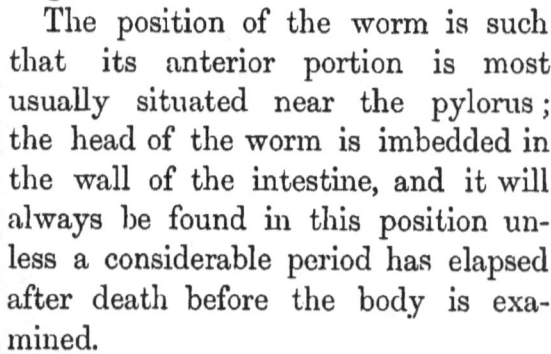

tænia solium, but when the worm is very long it may even extend into the large intestine.

The position of the worm is such that its anterior portion is most usually situated near the pylorus; the head of the worm is imbedded in the wall of the intestine, and it will always be found in this position unless a considerable period has elapsed after death before the body is examined.

This mode of attachment to the intestinal wall explains why the anterior portion, with the head, of the tænia is never dislodged by the unaided efforts of the intestine, although large-sized pieces are often expelled spontaneously after their separation from the head.

The tænia solium, as is implied by its name, is usually single; but cases are occasionally observed, in which two, three, or

[1] Fig. 13. Tænia Solium Armata (of the natural size). Fragments taken at certain distances between the head and the posterior rings, in order to show the successive form of these rings; the order of the letters indicates their arrangement from before backwards.

even more tæniæ exist at the same time in the same individual.

It is most usually met with in adults, but no period of life is completely exempt from it, and it has even been recorded in infants at the breast, or in very young children.[1] The age at which it is most frequently seen in European countries is from the fifteenth to the thirty-fifth year; in Abyssinia it is said to occur at all ages.

Females are more subject to tænia than males, the relative proportion between the two sexes being, according to some writers, nearly twice as great in the former as in the latter sex.

Some authors, judging from the circumstance that tænia is sometimes present in several members, both old and young, of the same family, have supposed that it may be transmitted hereditarily; but it would be more correct to conclude that several individuals in the same family, being exposed to the same errors in diet, may thus become affected with this entozoon.

It is also to some peculiarity connected with the manner of living that the so-called epidemics of tænia, which attacks a whole family, or several families residing in the same locality, ought probably to be attributed.

Persons who suffer from tænia pass, at intervals, considerable portions of the worm with the stools, either spontaneously, or as the result of the administration of anthelmintics; or else they void frequently, or even daily, some free, live segments (*cucurbitini*);

---

[1] For an explanation of this fact, see the note at page 57.

sometimes, also, the segments issue spontaneously during the intervals between the evacuations, and may be discovered in the clothes or in the bed of the patient.

The tænia is seldom ejected by vomiting, but several cases are recorded in which portions of tænia, or the cucurbitini, have been ejected through the mouth during the action of an emetic, or during a fit of coughing, caused probably by the reflex irritation produced by the passage of the tænia from the small intestine into the stomach.

The duration of the existence of tænia is sometimes very long, and instances of persons who have voided fragments of tænia during a continuous period of ten or twelve years are not rare. It appears very probable that in these cases several worms exist successively.

In the majority of the persons who suffer from tænia there exist a general indisposition, an anxious, restless manner, and more or less strongly-marked and persistent derangements of digestion, of nutrition, and of the nervous system. At first, they do not know to what cause the impairment of their health should be attributed, and they blame, in succession, various organs, especially the liver and stomach, until the expulsion of a portion of the tænia serves to show what their sufferings are due to.

The frequency, variety, and severity of the symptoms occasioned by tænia usually bear a marked relation to the constitution of the patient. They are more apparent in those men who are of a nervous temperament and of great susceptibility than in others ; and the symptoms are generally more numerous, more diversified, and more intense in females than in males.

The chief symptoms of tænia are :—Giddiness, confused noises in the ears, impairment of vision, itching at the nose and at the anus, increased flow of saliva, disordered appetite, indigestion, colic, pains at the epigastrium, and in other parts of the abdomen, palpitation of the heart, syncope, the sensation of some heavy substance in the abdomen which occasionally changes its position, weariness and pains in the limbs, and emaciation.

In some patients the morbid phenomena, particularly the peculiar sensation in the abdomen, the anxious, restless state of mind, and the faintness, come on during the day at regular periods, which have an evident relation to the hours at which the meals are taken, and which are removed after some food has been swallowed.

The abdominal pains which are caused by tænia, and which constitute its most frequent symptom, are similar sometimes to colic, sometimes to gastralgia ; and in other cases they are of a vague, indefinable character. They are situated in different parts of the belly, and in the loins ; they are more or less severe, and often sharp and intermittent, and are not ordinarily accompanied or followed by diarrhœa.

The itching at the anus is also one of the most common symptoms. In some instances it may be attributed, like the itching at the nose, which is less frequent, to sympathetic irritation ; but in the majority of cases it is due to the irritation of the mucous membrane of the lower part of the intestine by the contact and movements of the cucurbitini.

The appetite is often increased, and sometimes insatiable; at other times it is almost altogether wanting, or is subject to alternations of increase and of diminution.

There frequently exist, also, in persons who are affected with tænia, a feeling of general tenderness, lassitude, cramps, and pains in the extremities, which are often so severe as to prevent the patients from following their usual avocations.

The wasting is observable amongst persons who have suffered from tænia for a long period; tumidity and distension of the abdomen sometimes accompany this symptom.

The majority of these symptoms do not, for a time, usually cause any serious alteration in the health of the patients, but this is not the case with certain convulsive complications which are occasionally produced by tænia. These complications consist of more or less frequent attacks of convulsions, which present the characteristics of chorea, of epilepsy, or of hysteria.

Other sympathetic phenomena are sometimes seen amongst persons who are naturally nervous, or have become so in consequence of the illness caused by the tænia. These phenomena are very diversified in their nature, and depend upon the derangement of some sense or function. The most frequent are periodical rigors, muscular twitchings, obstinate cough, perversions of the sense of hearing, sight, or smell, hyperœsthesia or anæsthesia of various parts of the body.

Amongst the symptoms which have been mentioned, there is none which is decisively indicative of the existence of tœnia ; but when several of these phenomena are found united in the same individual, there are good grounds for suspecting its presence.

If the patient, in whom several of these symp-toms exist, has not already noticed fragments of tœnia in his evacuations, it will not usually be long before he discovers them, after his attention has been directed to this point ; for, as has been already stated, the passage of fragments of the tœnia, or of cucurbitini, occurs frequently and sometimes daily. It should, however, be borne in mind that the spon-taneous expulsion of tœnia does not take place in some cases excepting at intervals of several weeks, or even months, so that it will always be advisable to resort to the administration of an anthelmintic before a negative diagnosis can be given.

The complete expulsion of the tœnia generally causes a cessation of all the symptoms ; and that of a part of the worm causes their cessation for a period which is proportionable to the size of the portion which is expelled. When the head alone remains in the intestine, the symptoms do not re-appear until after several months.

CHAPTER VII.

THE BOTHRIOCEPHALUS LATUS.

LIKE the tænia solium, this worm inhabits the small intestine,[1] to the lining membrane of which it adheres by means of its head. It appears to be most frequent in adults and in females, but the conditions which attend its development are unknown.

The bothriocephalus may for a variable period be comparatively inoffensive, or it may soon give rise to marked symptoms, analogous to those produced by the tænia solium.

In order to complete the pathological account of this entozoon, it is only necessary to point out some slight differences which distinguish it from the tænia.

It usually attains to a greater length than the tænia, and sometimes assumes enormous proportions, so that the symptoms which it produces are often more severe than in the case of the latter parasite.

Its rings are not separately detached, and do not lead a distinct existence, after they have arrived at maturity; or, in other words, the bothriocephalus does not form cucurbitini.

The bothriocephalus is like the tænia commonly, though not always, solitary. Numerous cases have

---

[1] The tænia and the bothriocephalus, upon rare occasions, have been known to pass out through a fistulous wound in the intestine, but in such cases neither of these worms has had any influence upon the formation of the opening whence it has emerged; their heads which are buried in the mucous membrane of the intestine, do not cause any inflammation, or other appreciable change of the membrane, and cannot produce its perforation.

been recorded in which two or more bothriocephali have been expelled from the same individual; and, in the province of Nordbotten, in Sweden, where it is endemic, this worm seldom exists singly, according to Huss.

A frequent symptom of the tænia, namely, the itching at the anus, is not usually caused by the bothriocephalus; for, although it may, in the case of the latter worm, be produced sympathetically, like the itching at the nose, it is much less shown than the almost constant irritation which is dependent upon the movements of the cucurbitini, when the patient is affected with tænia.

The symptoms which especially denote the existence of the bothriocephalus are, according to Odier, of Geneva, whose opportunities of observation were very extensive, a tumid state of various parts of the abdomen, irregular evacuations, nausea, vertigo, palpitation of the heart, convulsive crying and sobbing during the night, cardialgia, and fainting.

In the province of Nordbotten, Huss states that the symptoms of bothriocephalus generally consist in an unpleasant sensation of suction at the epigastrium, especially when the patient is fasting, flatulent gurglings of the abdomen, and pain and tension around the orbits.

The duration of the bothriocephalus does not appear to be less than that of the tænia. Bremser records a case of this parasite which came under his notice, at Vienna, in a Swiss who had left his native country thirty years previously.

CHAPTER VIII.

ANCHYLOSTOMUM DUODENALE.

THIS entozoon belongs to the class of nematoid worms. It was discovered at Milan by Dubini, in 1838, but it has not been observed since then in any other part of Europe, although it has been frequently noticed in Egypt.

The anchylostomum only measures from about one-fifth to two-fifths of an inch in length, and its minute size may probably account for its not having been more generally observed. Its mouth is provided with a horny capsule, which is proportionately very large ; at the most prominent part of the margin of the mouth are situated four strong tooth-like processes, by means of which the animal attaches itself to the mucous membrane.

Dubini found this parasite chiefly during the months of May, November, December, and January, at Milan ; in Egypt it is so common that Bilharz and Griesinger met with it, sometimes only in small numbers, and at other times in hundreds, in the majority of the bodies which they examined. It inhabits the duodenum and jejunum.

According to Griesinger, the anchylostomum is kept firmly in position by the penetration of its head into the mucous membrane, and even into the subjacent tissue. The spot at which the worm is attached is marked by an ecchymosis as large as a lentil seed, and in its centre is found a white point of the size of a pin's head ; at this point the mucous membrane is perforated by a small opening, through which blood is freely effused into the intestine, which usually contains a considerable quantity of this fluid. The mucous membrane frequently presents a number of these ecchymoses, which are flattened, livid, and of a brownish colour ; they are caused by the accumulation of the blood which is effused between the mucous and the muscular coats of the intestine. The anchylostomum, having penetrated into the substance of the intestinal wall, is lodged within the cavity whence the blood is poured out.

According to the same author, the presence of this entozoon produces anæmia, in consequence of the small, but frequently repeated, hœmorrhage. He also states that the disorder, which is known as Egyptian Chlorosis, and which affects a large proportion of the population, is due to this cause ; but this has not yet been sufficiently established.

This malady, which is probably peculiar to African countries, attacks all classes of natives in Egypt. It is characterised, in the less severe cases, by the general pallor of the surface of the body, by palpitation of the heart, by increased frequency of the pulse, by lassitude upon the least exertion, and by disturbance of the digestive functions.

Its progress is ordinarily rapid, and it gradually goes on until decided marasmus is produced. The patient becomes very wasted, and weak ; and œdema of the lower extremities supervenes. The skin, which in the natural state is very tawny, assumes a pale yellowish or greenish tinge, and at the same time it is shrunken and cold. The conjunctiva is of a bluish white colour, and all the mucous structures, which can be seen, such as the lips, are of a deadly pale hue.

The other symptoms and complications of anæmia follow in quick succession; and the sufferer dies either of exhaustion, of dysentery, or of dropsy, accompanied by albuminuria.

Medical treatment alone, even when wine and powerful tonics are administered, often fails to check the progress of the disorder; and the hopes of a cure must depend chiefly upon a change of climate and of diet.

The morbid appearances which are found after death are serous effusions into different cavities, softening and discoloration of the muscles, general deficiency of blood, which is most evident in the brain, lungs, stomach, and mucous membrane of the intestines; the heart is pale, loaded with fatty deposition, and hypertrophied; the eudocardium and the valves of the heart are irregularly thickened; the liver is almost uniformly atrophied, whilst the spleen is much increased in size.

CHAPTER IX.

THE ASCARIS LUMBRICOIDES.

Synonyms:—Lumbricus Teres, Lumbricus Rotundus.

THE ascaris lumbricoides usually inhabits the small intestine. Sometimes it may get into the stomach, or the large intestine, but it soon perishes or is expelled from these situations. It may also find its way into cavities which possess a more or less direct communication with the alimentary canal, or, in consequence of the existence of a wound communicating with the intestines, it may reach parts which have naturally no relation to the intestines.

The number of lumbrici which are present in the same individual, at one time, is very variable; very often, not more than one or two, or from that number to six or eight, are found; whilst they are occasionally so numerous as to fill and even to distend the intestine; several cases are recorded, in which the lumbrici amounted to two or three hundred.

Children are more subject to lumbrici than adults, but these worms are rarely seen in children of less than one year of age; towards the age of three years these entozoa begin to become common. Women are said to be more frequently affected by them than men.

The ascaris lumbricoides is developed principally in persons who are of weak, scrofulous constitution, in those who live upon food of a bad quality, or who live chiefly upon legumes, fruit, and milk, or who do not drink fermented liquids, such as beer, wine, &c. The exact extent of the influence of constitution and of diet upon the development of worms has not, however, been yet determined.

The season of the year appears to exercise some influence upon the development of the round-worms, and most writers are agreed that these parasites are especially common in autumn; but this opinion has been sometimes based upon the importance which is attached to the use of fruits as a cause of the produc-

tion of entozoa.   It has also been observed that they
are frequent in the spring.

It has been generally supposed that the inhabitants of cold, damp countries are more subject to
lumbrici than people living in warm countries.   This
supposition is not, however, supported by facts ;
for although these worms are very common in Holland and in Sweden, which countries have been
mentioned in confirmation of the theory, they are
certainly not less frequent in tropical latitudes, as
has been shown by different observers in Brazil,
Cayenne, Jamaica, and elsewhere.

Again, if we consider that in some districts (the
province of Smaland, in Sweden, for instance) almost
every inhabitant is affected with lumbrici, it will be
evident that the influence of climate alone is small in
determining the frequency or rarity of these entozoa.
Besides this, as has been pointed out by Dr. Davaine,
the ascaris lumbricoides is comparatively rare in
Paris, whilst in some of the French provinces it is
very common ; the same comparison holds good with
regard to London and some parts of England, and
most probably depends upon certain local circumstances which favour the development of the lumbricus
in the rural districts.

According to the evidence of most authors upon
the diseases of negroes, they are much more subject
to round-worms than the whites are ; but no decided
reason has been given for this difference between the
two races.   Dyer, in the " London Medical Gazette "
for 1834, states his belief that it is due to the fact
that the negroes do not eat any salt, and Dazille
attributes it to their insipid, unfermented diet.

Under conditions which have not yet been satisfactorily determined, lumbrici may appear epidemically, or they may be endemically established in a certain district. The writers of the last century frequently refer to epidemics of fever or of dysentery, connected with the presence of entozoa.

When we endeavour to ascertain the conditions which determine the rarity of the ascaris lumbricoides in some localities, and its frequency in another, or its appearance in a large number of cases, epidemically as it were, it is especially requisite to recollect that this entozoon proceeds from an ovum, and that this ovum, after it has been expelled with the evacuations, must again enter the human intestine before it can become developed. It is consequently necessary to find out how the ovum is conveyed into the situation proper for its development. This is done, says Dr. Davaine, not by means of legumes, nor of fruit, nor of bad diet, but through the medium of the water which is used for drinking purposes. The ova of the lumbrici are expelled with the evacuations, which contain them in immense numbers. These ova may remain in the waters of a marsh, of a river, or of a well, during six or even more months without undergoing any change ; the embryo which becomes developed during this period is not set at liberty until the ovum again enters the human intestine. The use of a filter would separate the ovum from the water ; exposure to a high temperature would kill it.

With these data, it will be possible to account for the circumstance of these worms being so rare in large cities, which have a properly regulated supply of water, as compared with the rural districts ; in large towns the water is often passed through filters before it is distributed to the inhabitants, whilst in the country the unfiltered water of wells, and very often the impure water of brooks or of marshy places, forms the only means of supply. These wells or brooks are frequently fed by the rain-water which falls around the neighbouring houses ; and, as no system of sewerage exists, the water which is used for drinking purposes must necessarily become at times, and especially after heavy rains, contaminated with excrementitious matter, in which the ova exist.

Dr. Davaine's opinion, with which I fully coincide, serves to throw some light upon the cause of the epidemics which occasionally prevail in large armies during a campaign. It will also serve to explain the reason why negroes who are not over-delicate in their habits, and who drink the water which they obtain from any source nearest to their habitations, are so frequently affected with lumbrici, whilst the Europeans who reside in the same country, but who make use of fermented liquors imported from abroad, of tea, and of filtered water, enjoy a comparative immunity from these entozoa.

The age, temperament, and state of the health of a person may have some influence upon the development of lumbrici ; but it must be remembered that they do not occur spontaneously, and that the ova must be conveyed into the intestine before the lumbrici can be developed there.

Generally speaking, when the lumbrici are not very numerous, and when they still remain in their usual *habitat*, they do not give rise to any pain, nor to any appreciable functional disorder ; but when, on the contrary, they are present in large numbers, or have passed out of the small intestines into the stomach, or some other part, they occasion varied derangements in the digestive, nervous and other functions.

The symptoms which mark the existence of lumbrici in the intestine are similar to those which are indicative of other intestinal entozoa, and which have been already detailed in Chapter III. There are none which are peculiar to these worms, but those which are most frequently observed are :—Colic in the umbilical region, darting and tearing pains in the abdomen, which is more or less distended, depraved appetite, an increased flow of saliva, nausea, vomiting, dysenteric diarrhœa, and itching at the nose.

The following phenomena may also be sometimes observed :—Puffiness of the face, a leaden colour of the eyelids, unequal dilatation of the pupil, fœtor of the breath, emaciation, and certain nervous symptoms, such as confused dreams, grinding of the teeth and convulsive movements during sleep, wandering pains in the limbs.

No one of these symptoms, taken separately, is of much value ; but the joint appearance of several of them affords almost conclusive evidence of the existence of lumbrici in the alimentary canal.

Rosen states, in his work upon the diseases of children, that one of the surest signs of the presence of intestinal entozoa is the sense of relief which is experienced after a draught of cold water has been swallowed. Another author, Romans, states that the existence of small red, projecting, isolated, points at

the edges of the tongue is a pathognomonic characteristic of the presence of lumbrici in the intestines.
The expulsion of the lumbrici or of their ova, either
with the dejections or by vomiting, is the only sign,
however, which can be regarded as decisive.

The secondary affections which are produced by
lumbrici are, like those resulting from tænia, very
varied; sometimes they are strongly marked, and
they then become serious, and even mortal. This is
especially the case in countries where these worms
are endemic, and where they exercise a considerable
influence in modifying the characteristics of the other
disorders from which the natives suffer. Convulsive
attacks, speedily terminated by death, occasionally
occur, and these are so sudden and severe as to lead
to the suspicion of the administration of poison, until
a necropsy reveals the real cause. In the countries
referred to, lumbrici are so common that it is usual
to commence the treatment of almost every case of
acute disease by anthelmintics.

A considerable diversity of opinion exists amongst
writers upon the subject of entozoa, as to the extent
of the anatomical lesions which may be caused by
lumbrici. According to some, great laceration of the
mucous membrane of the intestine, and hœmorrhage,
may result from the numerous and repeated bites of
these worms, but these extreme views are not supported by post-mortem appearances. The changes
which are observed after death do not generally
amount to more than increased vascularity of the
intestine, and diminished thickness of the mucous
membrane at various parts; these changes are probably produced by the local irritation which is caused

by the worms ; upon rare occasions minute punctures, surrounded by a little red circle, have been found.

The lumbrici sometimes leave their usual situation either spontaneously, or in consequence of the expulsive efforts of the intestine, out of which they pass through either a natural or an accidental opening. When they pass out through a natural opening they find their way into a visceral cavity, or into some excretory duct which communicates with the alimentary canal, and when they emerge through an adventitious opening they find their way into some cavity which has no normal communication with the intestines, or else they get into the substance of the abdominal walls. In all of these cases, varied symptoms and serious complications result.

If worms be found in any organ, upon making a post-mortem examination, it is not to be always concluded that they must have existed there previously to the death of the patient ; as lumbrici live for several hours after the death of the individual who is affected by them, and their movements are sufficiently active to admit of their crawling out of the intestine along any passage where no actual obstacle is offered to their transit.

Lumbrici which have passed into the large intestines do not live there for any long period, and are commonly discharged with the evacuations without giving rise to any complications.

When they pass higher up the alimentary canal, and enter the stomach, they are usually expelled by vomiting ; their presence in this organ is generally borne with difficulty, and it excites pain, nausea, and vomiting.

Lumbrici which have passed through the stomach may be detained in the œsophagus; it is very probable, however, that they do not remain there long, but that they are speedily ejected by vomiting.

If they have happened to get into the pharynx, they produce great irritation, an uncomfortable sensation of constriction, and efforts to vomit, by which means they are commonly removed, unless they are soon extracted by the fingers; sometimes during the patient's efforts to vomit, they pass into the nasal fosæ, and escape through the nostrils. Besides the nostrils, the Eustachian tube, the frontal sinuses, the lachrymal duct, or the larynx may serve as a temporary refuge for the lumbrici, after their expulsion from the pharynx.

The number of well-authenticated cases of the entrance of lumbrici into the respiratory passages is very limited.

In addition to the circumstance that it is of importance to know that worms may occasionally be introduced into the larynx during life-time, so that prompt measures may be adopted for their extraction, in any case in which their existence is suspected, this fact is not without some value in a medico-legal sense. Dr. Davaine quotes the case of a woman who, although in good health on the previous night, v as found dead in her bed next morning; in the course of a post-mortem examination, an ascaris lumbricoides was discovered in the larynx, and the question was consequently raised as to whether such a worm could have entered the larynx during the life-time of the deceased.

In one-half of the recorded cases of the introduction of lumbrici in the air passages, the complication occurred in children between the age of four and ten years.

When a lumbricus has found its way into the larynx, it may remain entangled there, or it may pass beyond the glottis, and penetrate as far as the trachea or even the bronchi.

If it be only entangled at the upper part of the larynx, violent paroxysms of coughing, great anxiety, screaming, and pains at the situation of the larynx come on ; the suffocation becomes rapidly worse, and death occurs at the end of a short period, unless the worm be expelled during a fit of coughing.

When it has passed beyond the glottis similar symptoms are produced, but, as soon as the worm has completely entered the trachea or the bronchi, and has left the opening of the glottis free, the cough becomes less violent, and the sense of suffocation is less severe. The disorder continues, however ; the voice is stifled or suppressed, as well as the cough ; the patient places his hand up to his neck, as if to indicate or to attempt to remove the obstacle which opposes the free entrance of air into the lungs ; the dyspnœa recurs at intervals, and is accompanied by great mental agitation, vomiting, convulsions, and occasional involuntary discharge of urine. Death finally supervenes at a period which varies, according to published observations, from a few hours to three days, unless the worm be fortunately dislodged and ejected during the coughing. The symptoms cease almost immediately after the removal of the worm, either accidentally or by surgical means.

The diagnosis of the existence of a lumbricus in

the respiratory passages is very uncertain, as œdema of the glottis, croup, spasmodic laryngitis, and the introduction of any foreign body give rise to analogous symptoms.

The paroxysms of suffocation occasioned by œdema of the glottis and croup do not, however, come on suddenly, and without having been preceded, or being accompanied, by the general symptoms of a disorder of the larynx ; those of spasmodic laryngitis usually come on during the night, and occur in very young children ; the introduction of foreign bodies into the larynx takes place only during certain acts, such as that of swallowing food, of which the patient has generally some knowledge ; whilst the fits of coughing and of suffocation produced by the introduction of a lumbricus into the larynx may supervene at any moment, in individuals (especially children) who present the appearance of the most perfect state of health.

An examination of the throat and of the upper part of the larynx, either by the eye or by the finger, may probably assist in the recognition of the real course of the affection, if the worm (as has happened in nearly one-half of the recorded cases) be still partly in the pharynx.

It is scarcely necessary to observe that a lumbricus which is situated partly in the larynx, and partly in the pharynx, should be extracted as quickly as possible by the fingers, or by a forceps. When the worm is beyond reach, sternutatories and prompt emetics should be immediately administered, and if these should fail to dislodge the worm, tracheotomy should be performed.

Lumbrici may occasionally pass out of the intestine into the pancreatic, or the biliary ducts ; it is probable that in such cases the duct is more dilated than usual, either in consequence of abnormal enlargement, or else through some temporary cause, such as the passage of a gall-stone down the biliary ducts.

Lumbrici which have entered the biliary passages have been observed to be either contained partly within the ductus choledochus and partly within the intestine, or completely within the ductus communis choledochus, or the gall-bladder, or in the liver, where considerable changes of structure may have taken place owing to the irritation produced by the worm in that situation.

The presence of an ascaris lumbricoides in the biliary passages gives rise to various lesions ; it occasions or it maintains dilatation, and sometimes rupture, of the duct which it has invaded ; the dilatation may be either general, or else partial and limited to the portion of the duct which is occupied by the worm, which then appears as if it were contained in a special pouch. Neither the rupture of the duct nor the injury which is done to its internal surface, are attributable (as some say) to the suction of the lumbricus, but are due rather to the impediment which is offered to the passage of the bile, or else to the merely mechanical irritation which is produced by the presence of the worm, and is similar to that which would be caused by any other foreign body in the same situation.

Inflammation and suppuration usually occur when the worms have penetrated deeply into the biliary ducts, or into the structure of the liver. The pus m..y be discharged through the dilated duct ; or wl en the abscess has no direct or large-sized communication with the duct, the pus is retained, and, instead of the ascaris lumbricoides being contained in an empty and ulcerated cavity, it will be surrounded by a quantity of purulent matter. Sometimes the abscesses are numerous, as is the case in suppuration of the liver; these may communicate with each other, or be scattered throughout the entire mass of that organ, and they may become of considerable size, and extend towards the lungs, with which or with the the pleura a communication may be finally established. It may also happen that one of these abscesses may open externally, at the epigastrium, or in the right hypochondrium, and thus afford a means of exit to the lumbrici, whose passage through the substance of the liver would not be suspected, if it were not for the simultaneous escape of bile from the wound.

The symptoms produced by the presence of lumbrici in the biliary ducts are very variable ; and, although the affection of the liver may attract attention, the cause of it is not usually suspected. The most frequent symptoms which were observed in the cases which have been recorded were those of acute hepatitis, viz., pyrexia, pain in the hypochondrium, jaundice, convulsions, vomiting, and diarrhœa ; these symptoms were permanent in some cases, and came on in paroxysms in others.

The entrance of lumbrici into the biliary ducts must almost always be attended by grave consequences, as the probability of their return into the intestine is very small. Should they find their way back again into the intestine the real cause of the inflammatory symptoms which they had produced whilst in the ducts, might be suspected if the jaundice and other symptoms had disappeared suddenly, and if their disappearance had been accompanied, or soon followed, by the expulsion of a round-worm, either by vomiting or with the evacuations.

Lumbrici may also pass out of the intestine through passages which are accidentally formed, owing to gangrenous destruction or to ulceration of a portion of the intestine. After their escape from the intestine they may enter the cavity of the peritoneum, or one of the abdominal viscera, such as the bladder, or the substance of the abdominal walls, or some adventitious cavity ; or else they may arrive immediately at the exterior of the body, if the perforation of the intestine happen to communicate with a fistulous opening externally.

When the worms escape into the peritoneal cavity, peritonitis commonly supervenes, and the patient dies very shortly. The absence of these results in a few cases which have been recorded was most probably due to the circumstance that the lumbricus did not pass out of the intestine into the peritoneum until after the death of the persons in whom they were found upon a post-mortem examination.

When the lumbrici traverse the abdominal walls after leaving the intestine, they usually emerge at some point near to the umbilicus [1] or to the groin ; the

---

[1] The cases in which lumbrici have issued through the abdominal walls near the umbilicus have most frequently occurred in young children, a circumstance which serves to show the connec-

reason for this is that, owing to the intestines and the stomach being almost entirely surrounded by the peritoneum, there are only certain parts at which the worm can pass out of the intestine without getting into the peritoneal cavity, and this reason will also account for the fact that the number of cases which have been recorded of the passage of lumbrici into the peritoneum is very large, as compared with those cases in which the worms escaped by traversing the abdominal walls.

Sometimes, as a result of some lesion of the intestine, such as inflammation, ulceration, or gangrene, tumours are formed in which lumbrici are contained. The position of these tumours, which are usually situated near to the umbilicus or the groin, favours the inference that they most frequently result from strangulated hernia.

These tumours may be divided into three classes. In the first the worm, which has escaped from the intestine, appears to be the sole cause of the inflammation and suppuration of the parts which cover it. When the abscess is opened, pus of a healthy character issues from the opening, together with one or more worms, but no excrementitious matter; no fœcal fistula supervenes, and a speedy cure is effected.

In the second form, both the worms and the fœcal matter which have issued from the intestine take an equal part in the formation of the tumour; the opening remains fistulous for a variable period; and the discharge of fœcal matter, and sometimes of additional worms, furnishes a proof of the perma-

tion between this manner of exit and the relative frequency of hernia in different parts of the abdomen at different ages.

nence of the communication between the abscess and the intestines.

In the third class may be included those cases in which the worm does not reach the purulent abscess until after an external opening has been formed.

The cases which belong to the first class are rare. It has been attempted to explain them, upon the supposition that the lumbricus traverses the walls of the intestine by the division of the fibres which subsequently contract and close the opening through which the worm effected its passage. The absence of fœcal matter in the tumour which contains the worm may be explained in another way; a small ulceration may exist in a part of the intestine which is either not invested by peritoneum, or is attached to the abdominal walls by adhesions; the lumbricus may become entangled in this ulceration, and be conveyed into the neighbouring parts by following an oblique direction, similar to the course of the ureter between the coats of the bladder. It is said that in these cases the patient experiences in the tumour a peculiar quivering, pricking, or tingling sensation, and that crepitation may be felt upon a manual examination of the affected part. The symptoms, progress, and treatment of the tumour are similar to those of ordinary abscess.

The cases belonging to the second class are much more frequent, and have generally an evident connection with some primary lesion of the intestine; they usually occur in the inguinal or in the umbilical region. When the tumour is opened, spontaneously or by a bistoury, a means of exit is given to pus, fœcal matter, and worms which may be discharged either at once or at successive intervals. The wound degenerates into a fistulous opening which allows of the escape of fœcal matter; in some cases the fistula has been made permanent by the entanglement of lumbrici in it from time to time; the opening often heals spontaneously, and especially after the complete expulsion of the worms, according to some writers. In other cases closure of the fistula cannot be obtained; and death may result from the primary effects of the tumour, or in consequence of the protracted and exhaustive discharge from the chronic fistulous opening.

The treatment is that which is appropriate to abscesses of the abdominal walls; the application of poultices, incision with a bistoury, and simple dressings will be found most useful. If the wound has become fistulous, and still gives passage to worms, it is advisable to free the intestine from entozoa by purgatives and anthelmintics, as the lumbrici may, through their becoming entangled in the opening, keep up the irritation, and thus retard the cure. If notwithstanding the adoption of these measures the passage does not become closed, we must have recourse to the ordinary treatment of intestinal fistulæ.

The cases in which lumbrici which have had no share in the production of the tumour occasionally issue from the opening do not differ essentially from those which have been just described; and, frequently, the only distinction between them consists in the period at which the worms make their appearance externally.

Chapter X.

TRICOCEPHALUS DISPAR.

Synonym :—Trichuris.

THE tricocephalus has not been known for more than a century. It was first specially described during the epidemic of mucous fever, in 1760-61, of which Rœderer and Wagler have left an account ; it is probable, however, that this entozoon had previously attracted the attention of Morgagni. Rœderer and Wagler, supposing that the smaller end of this worm was the tail, gave to it the name of trichuris (from the Greek θριξ, genitive τριχος, a hair, and ουρα, the tail) ; but Goeze, who subsequently found that the small end was really the head, substituted for the original name that by which it is now generally known, tricocephalus (from θριξ, and κεφαλη, the head) ; the term " dispar " has been applied on account of the great dissimilarity between the size of the male and female of the species which occurs in man.

The tricocephalus dispar exists most commonly in the cæcum, and less frequently in the colon ; it is also sometimes found in the small intestines, but it has never been seen in the stomach.

A tricocephalus which was discovered in the tonsil of a man in the military hospital at Chatham has been referred to the tricocephalus affinis, a species which lives in the cæcum of the sheep and other ruminating animals ; but this was, perhaps, a tricocephalus dispar, which had been expelled from the intestines by the act of vomiting, and had lodged in the tonsil; it was found during a post-mortem examination of a soldier, who died at Fort Pitt; the left tonsil, in which it was embedded, was much enlarged, and in a gangrenous condition.

The tricocephali are probably fixed during life to the intestinal walls by their heads, which are thrust into the mucous membrane,

They exist in persons of all ages; Wrisberg states that he has seen them in children under two years of age, and they are known to be extremely common in adults. Many writers attest to their great frequency, and Dr. Davaine remarks that in making microscopical examinations of the dejections of a number of persons suffering from various diseases, he met with the ova of the tricocephalus in nearly one half of them.

These worms are usually not very numerous in the same individual, and sometimes only one or two specimens are found; but in certain affections, and especially in typhoid fever, they are discovered in greater numbers than in other diseases.[1]

This species of entozoon has been observed in all parts of the world; and especially in France, England, Germany, Egypt, and the United States.

Its mode of propagation appears to be analogous to that of the Ascaris lumbricoides. The ova, which are expelled with the evacuations, do not become

---

[1] Wrisberg affirms that these entozoa penetrate into the orifices of Peyer's glands, and of the mucous follicles in other parts of the intestines. This statement has been contradicted by some writers; but, if it be correct, it throws an important light upon certain morbid states of that portion of the intestines in which the tricocephali are found.

developed until some months afterwards in the water which has washed them from the soil; at a subsequent period they are conveyed by the water which is used for drinking purposes into the alimentary canal, where their shells are dissolved by the intestinal secretions, and the embryos are set free.

The symptoms which are produced by the presence of these worms in the intestines are almost unknown. Pascal, a French hospital physician, says, in a work upon this subject, that they give rise to the following pathological phenomena when they are very numerous :—Small, hard, irregular, and intermittent pulse, flushed face, prominence of the eyeballs, headache, and pinching pain in the abdomen ; these observations have not, however, been verified by any other writer.

There is no sign which can be considered as decidedly diagnostic of the existence of tricocephali in the intestines, as, owing to their tenacity of adherence to the mucous membrane they are not usually seen in the evacuations, excepting of persons who are affected with severe diarrhœa or dysentery ; the discovery of the ova would, of course, serve to complete the diagnosis.

Chapter XI.

OXYURIS VERMICULARIS.

Synonyms:—Ascaris (Hippocrates and Galen) ;
    Ascaris Vermicularis (Linnæus).
English common Name:—Small Thread Worm.

The oxyurides inhabit the large intestine and especially the rectum, in the lower part of which they
are commonly found ; they often emerge at the anus.

They generally exist in considerable numbers,
and are sometimes aggregated into a large mass.
Although they may be expelled by hundreds, either
spontaneously or as the effect of purgatives, they
may often be seen, at the end of a week or two, to
be apparently as numerous as before.

Children are much more subject to oxyurides
than adults are ; but persons may be affected by them
at all ages.

Nothing definite is known respecting the influence of diet upon the development of these entozoa ;
and that of the seasons is equally obscure. Several
writers state that they are more common in the
spring and autumn than at any other periods of the
year ; but these assertions appear to be based more
upon the theory referred to in the chapter upon the
Lumbrici than upon actual observation.

They have been met with in all European countries ; according to Bremser and Bilharz they are
very common in Syria and in Egypt ; they have also

been observed in Central Africa; and Leidy says that they are more common than any other species of worms amongst the white inhabitants of North America.

The presence of thread worms is, perhaps, more frequently discoverable by pathological phenomena, than that of the other intestinal entozoa. They usually produce a feeling of irritation in the rectum, lancinating pains, cramps, and acute, intolerable itching at the anus, or sometimes extending to the genito-urinary organs. These symptoms are greatly exacerbated at certain periods which vary according to the individual who is affected, or, it may be, according to the hours at which the meals are taken. The patients are commonly most tormented at the approach of night, and especially at bed time; and these sufferings return with such a degree of periodicity as can be explained only by their evident relation to the uniform performance of the digestive functions.

The patients are sometimes much depressed in spirits; and they suffer frequently from diarrhœa. Their evacuations are often soft, fetid, and covered with tenacious mucus, or streaked with blood.

It is generally easy to ascertain that these symptoms are due to the presence of oxyurides; some of these worms may be found in the folds of the sphincter ani, or in its immediate vicinity, and they are also expelled, at intervals, with the evacuations. Upon examination no cutaneous disorder is perceptible at the margin of the anus, but the mucous membrane which surrounds the sphincter is tumid, red, injected with blood, and covered with a thick, and sometimes sanguinolent mucus; it is studded with a multitude of small red spots which are due both to the irritation and to the bites of the oxyurides.

Although these means will usually suffice to prove the existence of oxyurides, it sometimes happens that they escape detection; in such cases their presence may be ascertained by the repeated administration of anthelmintics and purgatives, or by the employment of cold enemata.

Besides the general sympathetic complications, such as convulsions, chorea, epilepsy, &c., which may occur in a patient affected with any species of intestinal worms, oxyurides often produce local disorders of the genito-urinary organs; of these the most frequent are involuntary seminal emissions, and incontinence of urine; both of these disorders are due to reflex irritation.

The circumstance of the *habitat* of the thread-worms being in the inferior portion of the large intestines sufficiently explains why they are never expelled by vomiting, and also why they are not found in those viscera which are sometimes erratically invaded by lumbrici; the oxyurides seldom reach so high as the cæcum, and more rarely still in that part of the intestinal canal which is situated above the cæcum.

They frequently, however, issue from the anus, and are scattered about the perineum and the inner side of the thighs; in females, and especially in young female children, they may penetrate into the vulva and vagina. The oxyurides which have wandered into these situations produce violent itching,

acute inflammation, and obstinate leucorrhœal discharge, accompanied by redness and excoriation.   It
is highly probable that they do not live long after
having left the rectum.

CHAPTER XII.

THE TREATMENT OF INTESTINAL ENTOZOA.

THE various plans of treating the attacks of intestinal
entozoa may be divided into two classes, the preven-
tive and the curative.

The knowledge of the mode, or of the different
modes, of propagation of entozoa can alone furnish
the means of preventing their invasion of the body.
The recent progress of helminthology, by removing
the obscurity which attached to the origin of some
of these parasites, admits of some remarks being
made in this respect.

The ignorance which exists as to the manner in
which the bothriocephalus is transmitted necessarily
extends to the means for preventing its attacks.
Such is not the case, however, as regards the tænia ;
for one of the conditions, at least, of its development
are known, and it cannot be doubted that the proper
cooking of the meat, which is used as food, is the
reason to which the comparative rarity of this
entozoon in European countries must be assigned.

The ascaris lumbricoides and the tricocephalus
are developed externally to the body, in stagnant or

running water situated in the neighbourhood of human habitations, and it is through the agency of the water that the ova, which are already developed, are conveyed into the intestines ; the occurrence of these worms may be consequently prevented by the use of liquids prepared from fruits, or at a high temperature, such as wine, cyder, beer, and tea, by the proper cooking of the food, by the domestic employment of water which has been either filtered, or obtained from fresh, running springs, and, finally, by habits of cleanliness.

It is probable that certain states of the system favour the development of entozoa, just as they would promote that of external parasites, and it is a well-known fact that women and children are more frequently affected with worms than males and adults are. Entozoa do not spread amongst persons who are protected from the conditions which are favourable to their propagation ; just for the same reason that the itch, or pediculi, never attack an individual who keeps aloof from the contact of the parasites which occasion these diseases.

This remark does not, however, appear to be applicable to the oxyuris, which is reproduced in the intestine itself. Its presence, in some cases, seems to be maintained by a peculiar diathesis, and numerous cases have been recorded which show this. Dr. Davaine mentions the case of a man, nearly seventy years old, who, from the age of six years, had been obliged to take purgatives very frequently, in order to free himself from the constantly recurring attacks of this entozoon.

The curative treatment of intestinal entozoa

varies according to the species of worm, the part of the intestine which it inhabits, and the age and state of health of the individual who is affected.

The medicines which are used as anthelmintics act either as specific poisons to the parasites, or else as excitants of the secretions and of the movements of the intestines, by which the entozoa are expelled. All anthelmintics act generally upon several of the species of intestinal worms, but some possess a more marked effect upon particular species.

In the majority of cases these remedies are administered by the mouth; they are thus readily brought into contact with the entozoa which exist accidentally in the stomach, and with those which inhabit the small intestines and even the cæcum. Vermifuges have, however, a better effect if administered in the form of enema when the worms exist in the lower portion of the large intestine.

In the cases of very young children, and of those who, in consequence of some visceral affection, cannot tolerate anthelmintics when given internally, it will sometimes be found beneficial to apply them externally, either in the form of fomentations, or of ointments, or of baths. Santonine, tansy, absinth, and camphor are amongst the chief medicaments which may be used in this manner.

In extreme cases, as a last resource, the medicine has been injected into the veins. Dr. Davaine quotes an interesting case, under the care of Dr. Méplain, in illustration of this peculiar method of treatment.[1]

---

[1] A young woman, of twenty years of age, after some premonitory symptoms, fell into the following state :—There was complete immobility, the eyes were fixed, the pupils contracted,

With regard to the cestoid intestinal worms, considered separately, only a small number of remedies are now employed; with these remedies others more or less active are sometimes combined, or the patient may be subjected to some special preparatory treatment.

The medicines which are most used are the male fern, pomegranate bark, and kousso. These have been employed almost indifferently against the two kinds of cestoid worms; but the male fern appears to have a more certain action upon the bothriocephalus than upon the tænia solium.

It is very important, after the administration of the remedy, to make sure that the tænia or the bothriocephalus has been entirely expelled. Formerly, much value was properly attached to the expulsion of the head of the tænia; and as this worm is usually solitary, the cure is certain in the majority of cases, when the head has been discharged. Its expulsion is not, perhaps, so necessary now as it was formerly, because the remedies then in vogue were generally purgatives which drove the worm

the head was forcibly thrown backwards, and the mouth was convulsively closed so that it was impossible to get it open; there was also tetanic rigidity of the limbs, the breathing and pulse were scarcely perceptible, and there was total loss of sensation. As no remedy could be administered either by the mouth or *per anum*, and death appeared imminent, an injection containing four grains of tartarised antimony was passed into the median vein of the left arm. After an interval of half an hour, eight lumbrici, rolled up into a ball, and all living, were expelled by vomiting; the patient subsequently vomited seven more worms, at various times. All of the phenomena, which have been mentioned, speedily abated, and then disappeared, and in four days afterwards the patient was restored to perfect health.

from the intestines, but did not destroy it; whilst many of the anthelmintics which are employed at the present day have a toxic effect upon the parasite, so that if its anterior portion is not expelled, this is not of so much importance, as the vitality of the worm will most probably have been lost. The tænia can be expelled with less difficulty when the cucurbitini are detachable than at any other period.

The principal medicines which are employed in the treatment of the ascaris lumbricoides are semen-contra, santonine, and calomel. These should be given upon several days in succession, and their action should be assisted by the administration of purgatives.

After the use of the anthelmintics for some few days, we must judge by the presence or absence of the lumbrici or of their ova in the evacuations whether they have all been expelled, and whether we should continue or leave off the remedies. There is no reason to fear that fresh lumbrici will make their appearance if the patient is protected from the conditions which are favourable to the transmission of these entozoa.

The indefinitely prolonged use of anthelmintics with a view to the prevention of a recurrence of the lumbrici is useless, and might become injurious, as is also the case with regard to the other intestinal entozoa; it is consequently best to watch the state of the patient for a time, so that a second course of treatment may be resorted to, in the event of the reappearance of the worms.

When the tricocephali exist in the intestines, the best method of procuring their removal is the joint administration of medicines which serve to destroy the parasites, such as santonine, and of the more powerful purgatives, for the purpose of expelling the dead worms.

The treatment of the oxyurides consists in the administration of purgatives and of the vermifuges suitable for the destruction of the other nematoid worms; but these means will be insufficient in the majority of cases if the entozoa in the rectum be not also attacked by more direct means, such as injections of cold water, to which salt, an acid, or some empyreumatic oil, &c., may also be added, or by injections of the decoction of some fetid or bitter plant, such as that of assafœtida, or of absinth; the application of some anthelmintic or sedative substance in the form of ointment to the anus will be found occasionally useful in the removal of the oxyurides and in allaying the irritation produced by their presence. Lallemand recommends, as one of the best plans of cure, the use of injections containing sulphurous water.

The treatment ought to be continued for three or four weeks, or even longer, as it is necessary to destroy all the oxyurides as they issue from the ova, which are deposited in the substance of the mucous membrane, or in the secretion which covers it. Notwithstanding the most careful attention, this result cannot always be attained, and some persons are obliged to take occasional purgatives in order to keep themselves free from these troublesome parasites.

CHAPTER XIII.

AFFECTIONS PRODUCED BY THE PRESENCE OF ENTOZOA IN THE BILIARY PASSAGES.

THE fact that entozoa sometimes exist in the biliary passages was unknown to the ancients. Gabucinus, who, in a work published in 1547, mentions worms similar in appearance to gourd seeds, which he found in the livers of sheep and of goats, was probably the first observer of entozoa in the biliary ducts ; the worms of which he speaks were most likely a species of Distomum.[1]

Certain classes of animals are very subject to biliary entozoa, whilst others are wholly exempt from these parasites ; the herbivora, and especially rumi-

[1] The animal which is most subject to this species of worm is the sheep, in which the presence of the distomum hepaticum, or Liver Fluke, gives rise to the very destructive disease known as Watery Cachexia, or more commonly as the Rot. The great prevalence of this disease amongst sheep which are kept in wet, marshy meadows, and particularly where stagnant water abounds, points plainly to the means of prevention; and it has been practically shown that good and efficient drainage, with the occasional removal of the flock to a dry, upland pasture, suffices to maintain the sheep in a sound state upon farms where, previously to the drainage, it was impossible to graze sheep for many continuous weeks without their becoming affected with the rot. The impoverishment of the blood, in consequence of large quantities of serum being drained away by the bowels, brings on a dropsical condition, of which the sheep eventually dies. The great importance of this disease will be understood, when it is stated that the author of the "Treatise on the Sheep," in the "Library of Useful Knowledge," estimates the yearly mortality from it at one million of sheep and lambs in this country alone.

I

nant animals, come under the former head, and the carnivora, with the exception of the domestic cat, may be included under the second.

In man and in the domestic animals the entozoa which live in a free state in the biliary ducts belong to the Trematoda, and also, almost exclusively, to the genus Distomum ; there are also found in the biliary passages of the rabbit, and have been once observed in a corresponding situation in man, by Gubler, masses of oviform bodies, the origin of which is unknown, but which bear a strong resemblance to the ova of worms.

The nematoidea which have been sometimes observed in the gall-bladder and bile ducts are intestinal worms which have wandered from their usual *habitat ;* the hydatids of the liver may also accidentally get into these ducts in consequence of a perforation of their walls, which brings them into relation with the hydatid cyst.   The intestinal entozoa have been already described.

The cases of distoma which have been observed in man are rare.

Bucholz found a large number of these entozoa in the gall-bladder of a prisoner, who had died of fever, at Weimar.   According to Rudolphi, who quotes this case, with some others, the worms seen by Bucholz belonged to the species Distomum lanceolatum.

More recently, the discovery of the distomum hepaticum in several cases has been recorded by various writers, including Mr. Busk and Mr. Partridge in England.

In Mr. Busk's case the distoma, fourteen in number, and averaging from one and a-half to nearly three inches in length, had left the biliary passages and were found in the duodenum; the patient was a Lascar, who died in the "Dreadnought" hospital ship.

With respect to the treatment of these entozoa when they occur in man, little can be said. It is not probable that their existence would be suspected, as they do not produce any special symptoms; but this is not of much moment, as the treatment which is usually adopted in hepatic diseases is that which would be the most likely to lead to the expulsion of the parasites.

When they have wandered from their original *habitat*, and are contained within the duodenum, they can be expelled by the medicines which are employed in the treatment of intestinal worms.

CHAPTER XIV.

AFFECTIONS OF THE URINARY ORGANS PRODUCED BY ENTOZOA.

THE urinary organs in man are very rarely affected by entozoa, and only one species of worm, viz., the strongylus gigas, appears to be peculiar to these parts.

The cases which have been recorded of parasites which have been observed in the kidneys or in the bladder, and which do not belong to the strongyli, relate to:—1. The protozoa; 2. Worms whose species was not determined, and which have only been

observed once, or twice at the most; 3. Intestinal or
hydatid worms which had wandered from their usual
habitat; and 4. Vermiform bodies which were not,
perhaps, living animals, but were fibrinous concretions
formed in the urinary passages, or insects, or the larvæ
of insects which had accidentally fallen into the urine.

The strongylus gigas, which has been frequently
observed in the dog, horse, ox, and some other animals, usually inhabits the kidney both in them and
in man; it is probable that it at first occupies the
calyces or the pelvis, and it is seldom found in the
ureter, or in the bladder; only one kidney is commonly affected.

It rarely happens that there are more than two
strongyli in the same person, and generally only one
is met with.

The existence of a strongylus in the kidney gives
rise to serious functional derangements; the substance of the organ is gradually destroyed, and the
vessels which, for a variable period may resist the
destructive process, are subject to frequent hœmorrhage.   The worm is usually involved in a sanguinolent
mass, and a large tumour is formed by the renal
capsule, within which the sanguinolent, or sometimes
purulent, fluid and the strongylus are contained;
when the fluid consists chiefly of pus, the entozoon
loses its ordinary red appearance, and assumes a
whitish colour.   The capsule of the kidney becomes
misshapen and thickened, besides undergoing further
changes which are not yet understood.

The kidney, which is situated upon the healthy
side of the body, acquires a bulk which is much
greater than the normal size; this alteration being

doubtless due to the circumstance that the function of eliminating the urine is transferred, and almost entirely limited, to the unaffected kidney.

According to the cases which have been observed, a peculiar undulatory movement which is felt only in one renal region, is diagnostic of the presence of the strongylus gigas.   Sometimes these movements produce violent pain in the loin ; and, as long as the ureter remains permeable, sanguinolent or purulent urine is voided.   When it has escaped into the ureter, it causes retention of urine and enlargement of the kidney ; when it has arrived into the bladder, it gives rise to various complications analogous to those which are caused by the existence of other foreign bodies in this viscus.

Many of these symptoms resemble those which are present in cases of renal calculi ; but, as Dr. Davaine observes, the diagnosis may be completed, in a suspected case of strongylus, if the ureter remains permeable, by a microscopical examination of the urine, which may lead to the discovery of the ova of the entozoon.   These are of an oval shape and brownish colour, and are very abundant ; they measure $\frac{3}{1000}$th of an inch in length, and about half of this in breadth.

When the nature of the ova has been fully determined, and the symptoms of a foreign body in the kidney or in the bladder also show that a strongylus exists in one of those viscera, incision into the kidney will be indicated when it is in that viscus, if the worm cannot be dislodged by diuretics, and it will be advisable to remove the entozoon from the bladder, when it is in that situation, by means of lithotrity instruments.

No protozoa are found in the healthy urine, and they are also very seldom met with even in morbid states of that secretion. Vibriones and monades are the only protozoa which have been hitherto observed; the former in a case of chronic cystitis, and the latter in several cases of persons suffering from cholera, during the epidemic which prevailed in London in 1854.

The following species of entozoa have been each observed once in the urine :—The Spiroptera hominis, in a case recorded by Mr. Lawrence ;[1] the Dactylius aculeatus, described by Mr. Curling ;[2] the Tetrastomum renale, observed by Delle Chiaje ;[3] besides which Wagner states that he has found the Pentastomum denticulatum imbedded in the substance of the kidney.[4]

Hydatid and intestinal worms also, sometimes accidentally find their way into the urinary organs.

The intestinal entozoa which have been expelled with the urine are the tænia, the ascaris lumbricoides, and the oxyuris. The latter worm may possibly reach the bladder sometimes, through the urethral

---

[1] This case is given at full length in the " Medico-Chirurgical Transactions " for 1812.

[2] For full account of this case, see " Medico-Chirurgical Transactions " for 1839.

[3] Delle Chiaje, " Compendio di elmintografia humana," Naples, 1833. As the entozoa described by this author were found only in the urine, and not in the kidneys, the designation *Renale* was simply given upon the supposition that the kidney is the normal *habitat* of this species.

[4] " Archiv. für Physiologie," von Vierordt, 1856.

canal, in the female ; but the others can only get
into the urinary organs through an accidental
opening, such as that of an abscess of the kidney,
communicating with the intestines.

The peculiar characteristics of these worms are
sufficient to show their origin.   When they occur in
the urine, it is necessary to ascertain the situation of
the injury by which they have penetrated the bladder.
The knowledge of the symptoms and progress of the
affection, the inspection of the matters discharged
from the urethra, the examination of the part by
means of a finger passed into the rectum, or of a
sound introduced into the bladder, and an injection
thrown into the latter organ, will form the means of
diagnosis.

The treatment of the vesico-intestinal fistula
should be accompanied by the administration of an
anthelmintic, in order that the intestines may be
freed from the entozoa, whose passage into the fistula
might frustrate any plans adopted for its cure.   The
use of injections of cold water into the bladder has
been attended with success.

The hydatids which are occasionally found in
relation with the urinary organs will be described in
a future chapter.

Chapter XV.

THE ENTOZOA FOUND IN THE SANGUINEOUS SYSTEM:—HŒMATOZOA.

THE existence of worms in a free state in the blood-vessels of certain animals is a fact which has long been recognised ; and these parasites have been united into a distinct group, and described under the name of Hœmatoza.

They have been found in mammiferæ, in birds, reptiles, fishes, and several invertebrate animals. The majority of them are of microscopical size, and circulate with the blood through the vessels ; a few species only are provided with reproductive organs, and attain to more considerable dimensions, and these are generally confined to special parts of the sanguineous system.

Their origin is, like that of many of the other entozoa, not yet known. Even if we suppose that those which possess reproductive organs are developed in the cavity which they inhabit, the question will arise how they are transmitted from one person to another, and also why it is that their number is usually limited, although their ova or their larvæ may exist in considerable quantity.

Some observations which have been recently made tend to show that some of the species of hœmatozoa which are unprovided with reproductive organs are the larvæ of worms which live either in the vessels or in the viscera of the animal in which they are found.

In Europe no entozoon is known which has its normal *habitat* in the blood-vessels of man; but in Egypt a trematode worm, discovered in 1851, and belonging to the genus Distomum is frequently found in the abdominal veins.

It exists in the portal, mesenteric, splenic, intestinal, and visceral veins; it does not appear to produce any serious disorder of the principal trunks of those vessels, but it causes grave complications when it is contained in the capillaries of the mucous membrane.

When this hœmatozoon (the distomum hœmatobium) is situated in the vessels of the walls of the bladder, it gives rise to marked structural lesions. The mucous membrane is swollen, and is studded with numerous circumscribed spots, considerably injected with blood, which is also extravasated in large quantity, or the membrane is covered with tenacious yellowish masses of exuded mucus, in which the ova of the worms are imbedded. In more advanced stages, the exudations and partial ecchymoses are increased in size and in number; and the discoloured elevations, together with the extravasated blood, frequently form a soft coat, which is so firmly connected with the mucous membrane, that when it is detached part of the membrane is removed with it. The ova of the worms sometimes give a sandy appearance to the urine.

The mucous membrane of the ureter, and in some rare cases that of the pelvis of the kidney also, are affected similarly to the corresponding investment of the bladder; and the aggregation of the ova, exudation corpuscles, and crystals of uric acid, forms

a soft adherent coating, of a dark colour, and roughened feel. As a result of this thickening, stricture
of the ureter occurs, and is followed by dilatation
above the contracted portion of the tube, and retention of urine. The kidney is usually swollen and
filled with blood; and is subject to fatty degeneration
after the disease has lasted for some time. Pyelitis,
and fan-like dilatation of the renal pelvis and calices,
with atrophy of the substance of the kidney, sometimes supervene. The aggregation of the ova occasionally serves as the nucleus of depositions of gravel,
and of calculi, consisting chiefly of lithic acid.

Changes of structure similar to those described in
the bladder take place when the intestinal mucous
membrane is affected by hœmatozoa.

The trunk of the portal vein is sometimes found to
be filled with mature distoma, and their ova are even
contained in the liver; under such circumstances,
the texture of the liver is considerably altered, and
hepatic abscesses are formed.

When there is hœmaturia without any evident
cause, and when the general symptoms of an affection
of the bladder, or kidney, have attracted attention,
an examination of the urine, for the ova of the
distoma, will often afford certain proofs of the
existence or of the absence of these worms.

Our present state of ignorance concerning the
manner in which hœmatozoa are developed and
transmitted, does not admit of our ascertaining the
means of preventing their invasion. With respect
to the curative treatment which should be adopted,
little is known; empyreumatic or fetid remedies,
such as turpentine and assafœtida, would most pro-

bably have the same effect upon these worms as upon other entozoa.

In some few cases the distomum hepaticum has been found in the abdominal veins, into which it has accidentally entered.

Treutler has described two trematode worms, which he observed in a wound communicating with the anterior tibial artery; he considered these as belonging to a distinct species, to which he gave the name of Hexathyridium venarum, but it appears highly probable that they were only the young of the distomum hepaticum, or of the distomum lanceolatum.

Chapter XVI.

GENERAL REMARKS UPON THE ENTOZOA WHICH EXIST IN NATURAL OR IN ADVENTITIOUS SEROUS CAVITIES.

THE cavities which are invested by a serous membrane may be affected by entozoa, as well as those cavities which are provided with a mucous membrane. These entozoa belong to the nematoid and to the cestoid classes of worms; the nematoid worms are found only in animals, and especially in the horse.

The cestoid entozoa which are found in the serous cavities are vesicular worms which, in consequence either of their number, or of their bulk, give rise to marked derangements, or even to serious secondary affections.

The natural serous cavities are not all equally

liable to the attacks of vesicular worms, which have not been met with in the synovial cavities, or in the peritoneum, in man, unless they happen to have reached the latter cavity accidentally, owing to the rupture of a cyst situated in one of the abdominal viscera.

The cavities in which vesicular worms have been observed in a free state in man are the cerebral ventricles, the arachnoid membrane, the chambers of the eye, the pleura, the pericardium, and the tunica vaginalis testis.

Although this enumeration suffices to show that vesicular worms may live in a free state in most of the natural serous cavities, they are not very often found in these situations, especially in man; and it is, in fact, in the parenchymatous organs that they most frequently make their *habitat;* they are, however, separated from the tissue composing these viscera by an adventitious pouch or cyst, whose structure is analogous to that of a natural serous membrane.

In whatever part of the body the vesicular worms may be developed, they possess no action upon the viscus in which they are contained except indirectly, through the medium of the membrane which encloses them, and this action presents no difference, whether they are contained within a natural or an adventitious cavity, as the effects produced by these entozoa are only those which result from compression.

The lesions which are produced by the existence of hydatids in man will be first discussed; and, subsequently, those which are produced by the presence of cysticerci.

Chapter XVII

HYDATIDS IN MAN.

The Anatomical Constitution of Hydatid Tumours, and the Changes which they undergo.—The Chemical Composition of these Tumours.

The hydatids in man, when in a perfect condition, are rounded vesicles, formed of a substance similar to coagulated albumen, which are free from any adhesion to the tissue of the viscus which conceals them. They enclose a limpid fluid, and generally contain echinococci, which are either attached to the internal surface of the vesicles, or float at liberty in the hydatid liquid.

The hydatids which are found in man are of a very variable size ; sometimes they are scarcely perceptible to the naked eye, and in other cases they attain to the dimensions of the head of a fœtus at the full period of gestation.   In the majority of instances, their size ranges from that of a pea to that of an orange.

Their form, which is primitively spherical or oval, is occasionally modified in a permanent manner by the pressure of the surrounding parts which oppose some obstacle to their regular development.

Their walls are generally of an uniform thickness, proportioned to the size of the vesicle, and they are colourless and transparent, or of an opaque tint at various parts of their extent.   Accidental circumstances, such as the contact of a coloured fluid, of the bile for example, give rise to change of colour.

The substance of the hydatid is homogeneous, friable, elastic, destitute of fibres or cells, and analogous in its appearance and consistence to the boiled white of an egg. This substance constitutes a membrane which is arranged in stratified layers ; these layers, which are extremely fine, are evident, even in the smallest hydatids, upon a microscopical examination, and form a distinctive character of this pathological product.

Although they are smooth and even externally, hydatids often present numerous irregularities on their internal surface. The smallest hydatids are constituted like the largest, as regards their walls ; and if they are not very small, the existence of a central cavity can also be ascertained. The cavity contains a more or less abundant liquid, which is ordinarily serous and limpid. It is lined, in the *fertile* hydatids, by a special membrane (the *germinal membrane*), from which the echinococci arise.

Sometimes several small hydatids are found in company with a large one, to which they are external, and, more frequently still, a large hydatid encloses several smaller ones, which float freely within its cavity ; or numerous small ones may be found adherent to either the external or the internal surface of a large one. These hydatids arise, like buds, from the substance, or on the surfaces, of the envelopes of the parent hydatid, form elevations upon these surfaces, and after growing and becoming hollow, are finally detached.

Those hydatids which are much distended by fluid possess remarkable elasticity, so that the least shock to any part is transmitted through the whole mass, and occasions a peculiar, prolonged trembling motion, which, in some cases, forms a means of diagnosis of this class of tumours.

The periods during which the hydatids live is uncertain, but it is probably rather long, as even in tumours which are of considerable duration, some of the hydatids may be found to be unaltered ; more frequently, however, they will be found to have undergone some changes. The echinococci which they contain may almost entirely disappear, and the hooklets which remain will then furnish the only indication of their previous existence ; the membrane of the hydatid may have lost more or less of its transparency and of its homogeneity, in consequence of the development of apparently fatty granules in its substance ; the membrane may also have become collapsed, but the liquid which it contains usually preserves its limpidity ; sometimes the membrane is ruptured, and its cavity is then completely effaced. It may also happen that all the hydatids contained within a cyst lose their fluid simultaneously ; the vesicles then collapse and are folded together, whilst the cyst undergoes a proportional contraction, until eventually the latter only contains the membranes folded together, like the petals of a poppy enclosed within the calyx.

The substance of the hydatid resists absorption or total transformation for a very considerable period ; so that even in the oldest hydatid tumours there may be found membraneous shreds and the hooklets of the echinococci, which afford evidence of the primitive character of the tumours.

As has been already mentioned, the hydatids

which are developed in parenchymatous viscera are enclosed in a cyst which isolates them from the surrounding tissues. This cyst is formed by the areolar tissue of the viscus in which the vesicular worms are contained, and does not appear to differ from that which becomes developed around any other foreign body in a similar situation; it presents certain differences of structure which bear an evident relation to the nature of the viscus in which it originates; thus, for example, it is thick and firm in the liver, but very delicate and of only slight consistence in the brain.

The hydatids which are developed in a natural serous cavity have no special pouch, and the reason for this is, doubtless, that they find in the membrane which lines such cavities conditions of structure analogous to those of areolar cysts.

The walls of hydatid cysts are composed of areolar tissue, which is more or less condensed, and arranged into layers which may be separated into strips of variable size, but not into distinct tunics.

Besides the differences which these walls present according to the various organs in which they are situated, other differences may also be observed which bear a relation to the age and to the natural growth of the bodies which they contain. The thickness of the walls increases in proportion to the size which the tumour acquires, and, still more perhaps, in proportion to the duration of the tumour. Although it is thin and simply areolar at first, the cyst becomes subsequently strong and dense, and, at a still later period, it acquires the consistence of fibrous tissue, or even of fibro-cartilage. Cretaceous deposits may be frequently found scattered throughout the substance of old cysts ; these deposits have a bony appearance, and are composed of phosphate, together with a small proportion of carbonate, of lime. They do not invade the walls of the tumour in an uniform manner ; sometimes the walls are thin and almost transparent in certain parts, and thick and fibro-cartilaginous in others; whilst in other instances, again, they may have become almost completely osseous. As has been pointed out by Dr. Budd, there is a greater tendency to the deposition of earthy matter in the cysts which occur in old people than in those which occur in younger persons.

The cyst may become united to the adjacent parts, sometimes by very loose areolar tissue, with blood-vessels ramifying in it, and sometimes by con-densed fibrous tissue, which forms firm adhesions, which can only be destroyed with much difficulty.

When the hydatids are developed upon the sur-face of an organ, in the sub-serous areolar tissue, it may happen that the cyst pushes aside the serous membrane, by which it is partially invested, and that it only remains held in relation with its point of origin by a more or less elongated and slender stalk.

The internal surface of recent hydatid cysts is white, and smooth, and resembles, to a certain extent that of a serous membrane ; in old cysts, it is roughened, and covered with thick exudations, whilst the vessels sometimes present a varicose appearance, or are surrounded by sanguineous effusions.

The hydatid cyst is generally of a globular form, and either smooth, or irregularly nodulated, but it is rarely composed of distinct cells ; this latter appear-

K

ance may result from the fusion of several cysts. When the hydatid pouch is multilocular, in consequence of the obstacles which are opposed to its uniform increase in size the hydatid, if it is entire, sends prolongations into the various cells, as has been pointed out by Cruveilhier.

In Man, a cyst frequently encloses several hydatids; their number may be very considerable, amounting sometimes to beyond a thousand. When the hydatids are very numerous, the tumour always attains to enormous dimensions.

When the cyst only contains a single hydatid, the latter usually completely fills it up, and lines its walls; when it contains several, some fluid in which the hydatids float is found within its cavity. This fluid is either transparent and limpid, like that which exists in vesicles, or it may be variously coloured, turbid, and thick.

It has already been stated that hydatids have a limited existence, and that they are sooner or later destroyed, together with the echinococci which they contain. This destruction is probably caused by the action of the pouch which encloses them; at any rate, the entire mass of the tumour presents morbid changes which do not appear to commence with the hydatids themselves.

When the vesicular worm is solitary, or when, being multiple, these worms have their vesicle attached to the cyst without the interposition of fluid, a substance of a tubercular or fatty appearance, and which is semi-liquid and viscid, or thick and firm, is deposited in layers upon the internal surface of the cyst; this substance accumulates, and completely envelopes the hydatid vesicle, or else presses it against one side of the pouch. The liquid contained in the hydatid usually remains limpid, but it diminishes in quantity, and the vesicle collapses ; at the same time, the cyst contracts, and thus contributes to the further effacement of the cavity.

In the course of time the secreted matter thickens, becomes harder, and assumes the appearance of painter's putty, and occasionally that of chalk ; the hydatid is reduced to a few membranous shreds and finally disappears ; the only traces of echinococci, which are also destroyed, are their hooks.

In other cases, the hydatid tumour undergoes changes which are different in appearance, although of a similar character ; the substance which fills up the cyst is fluid, and resembles pus or softened tubercle. The matter contained within the cyst may also have a reddish, yellow, or greenish tint, in consequence of its admixture with the animal fluids, such as blood or bile.

The knowledge of the chemical composition of the hydatid membrane is comparatively unimportant, but such is not the case with respect to the composition of the liquids, or of the matters which they enclose.

The hydatid liquid contains only traces of albumen, and no phosphates ; but it holds in solution a considerable amount of chloride of sodium, the crystals of which become evident under the microscope when a drop of the fluid has been placed upon a piece of glass, and allowed to evaporate. Its specific gravity is from 1·008 to 1·013 ; and it is either neutral or slightly alkaline. It is not coagulable by heat nor by acids.

The atheromatous substance found in old hydatid cysts is composed principally of phosphate of lime, and of an animal matter similar to albumen; it also contains a small quantity of carbonate of lime, of cholesterine, and other fatty matters. The presence of cholesterine in the cysts which have become atheromatous is probably general.

Other substances, the presence of some of which is accidental, are also occasionally found in hydatid cysts. These are hœmatin, sugar, and some of the urinary salts.

All of the tumours in which the colouring principle of the blood (hœmatin) has been observed, have occurred in the liver; and it is in the fluid contents of tumours in this situation that the existence of sugar has been noted. The urinary salts were found in some hydatid cysts which were voided with the urine; they consisted of the crystals of uric acid, oxalate of lime, and phosphate of soda, and their presence was attributed by Mr. Quekett, who examined the cysts, to the penetration of the urine through the walls of the cysts by endosmosis.[1]

----

[1] Cruveilhier has readily shown the permeability of hydatids, by placing them in ink. The liquid which they contain soon becomes blue, and then black.

Chapter XVIII.

The usual Seats of Hydatid Tumours.—The Circumstances which regulate their Development and Frequency.—The Changes in neighbouring Organs, produced by their presence.—The Diagnosis, Prognosis, and ordinary Termination of Hydatid Tumours.

Hydatids are found in all of the parenchymatous viscera in Man, although with a very different degree of frequency; the liver alone furnishes more cases than all of the other organs taken together. When hydatids do exist in some distant parts of the body, they may often be, at the same time, met with in the liver; next to this organ come the lungs, in respect to the frequency of hydatids; vesicular tumours are also occasionally present in the spleen, the kidneys, the omentum, and the brain; some few examples have been recorded in the spinal cord, the eye, and even in bones; hydatids are seldom seen in the extremities or in the parietes of the chest and of the abdomen; the testicle, the uterus, and the mammæ are very rarely affected by them.

The hydatid cyst is often single, but it is not, however, unusual to see two, three, or four cysts in the same organ, or in various regions of the body; their number seldom exceeds ten or twelve, although, in some instances, more than fifty and even as many as a thousand, have been observed.

The tissues or the viscera in which hydatid cysts are developed may remain for a long time without experiencing any appreciable change. At a subsequent period, however, they often become more or less atrophied, and may even completely disappear in consequence of the continuous development of the foreign body which presses upon them. They may also undergo considerable alterations in their structure, at least in that portion which is in immediate relation with the hydatid, and which may become condensed, and be entirely metamorphosed in its constitution. The neighbouring viscera contract firm adhesions with that which contains the cyst, and are sometimes involved in similar structural changes.

That part of the organ which is not in relation with the cyst generally remains healthy; with the exception, sometimes, of an increase in size. Dr. Davaine states that he has observed, in several cases of large hydatids of the liver, a granular state of that portion of the parenchyma which has remained sound; he thinks that this is not connected with cirrhosis, but that it is probably due to hypertrophy of certain elements which exaggerate the healthy granular appearance of the hepatic tissue; and he proceeds to suggest that in those parts which escape the pressure of the cyst there would be produced an hypertrophied condition analogous to that which occurs in one of the kidneys, when the other kidney is destroyed.

In some cases, in consequence of external or other injury, an inflammatory action is set up in the parts in the vicinity of the cyst, and diffused purulent depositions, usually of a small bulk, are formed. It is doubtful whether the internal wall of the hydatid pouch ever spontaneously becomes the seat of suppuration. Instances have been recorded in which the suppurative process attacked the veins of the affected organ, and the inflammation extended to distant viscera; but it is probable that this complication only arises subsequently to the accidental communication of these vessels with the cavity of the cyst.

In other cases, the parts which are in relation with the hydated pouch are destroyed and ulcerated, as well as the corresponding wall of the pouch, which is thus perforated and affords a means of exit to the matters which it encloses; the hydatid cyst, under such circumstances, opens directly upon the surface of the body, or into some passage which has a more or less direct communication with the exterior of the body, such as the bronchi, the intestinal canal, the biliary tubes, and the urinary passages, or else into a closed cavity, like the pleura, the peritoneum, or even the veins. In this manner, the tumour is sometimes brought into communication with some distant organ which has ordinarily no connection with that in which the hydatids are contained; cysts situated in the liver, for instance, after the diaphragm and the pulmonary tissue have been perforated, occasionally open into the bronchi, through which their contents are finally discharged.

It is not upon the soft parts alone that the pressure of hydatids exerts a destructive influence; for, when they are in relation with a bone, they may give rise to absorption and perforation. Andral relates the case of a patient in whom acephalocysts primarily developed in the sub-scapular fossa, made their way through the shoulder-blade into the sub-spinous fossa.

A communication may be established between two hydatid cysts by the perforation of both. The cases which are recorded of hydatid tumours containing several cells separated from each other by imperfect septa are not very rare, and these cells may have been produced by the union of several cysts, whose walls have been perforated at the point of contact.

Hydatids exist principally at the middle period of life, being most common in persons from twenty to forty years of age ; they are almost unknown in young children.

They do not appear to be of more frequent occurrence in one sex than in the other.

It is not conclusively known whether various occupations have any influence upon the frequency of vesicular worms ; it has been remarked by Dr. Budd and Mr. Busk, of the " Dreadnought " hospital-ship, that hydatids are apparently very rare amongst sailors, and it is possible that the diet of seamen, which consists for the most part of salted provisions, may be unfavourable to the development of these entozoa.

According to Dr. Budd, the poorer classes in England are more often affected with these worms than the rich are ; and he thinks that this circumstance may be accounted for by the fact that the poor live in damp, badly-drained houses, and that their diet is less nourishing and composed chiefly of vegetables. It is well known that hydatids are very common in sheep and in cattle which graze in marshy pastures, and especially during rainy seasons. The influence of diet upon the production of vesicular worms is therefore tolerably manifest, but its mode of action is as yet almost completely hidden in obscurity.

The question has been suggested why these entozoa are usually situated in the abdominal and thoracic viscera. A plausible explanation of this fact may be obtained, if it is true that hydatids, as has been advanced by some writers, owe their origin to the transformation or to the development' of the embryo of a tænia. This embryo, having been introduced into the alimentary canal with the food or with the drink, and being unable to live or to develop itself in the intestine before it has undergone certain metamorphoses, quits the intestine, and reaches the adjacent viscera, either directly or else indirectly, through the medium of the blood-vessels.

In some countries, as for example amongst the white population of North America, vesicular worms are very rare, whilst in others they are very common. In Iceland hydatids prevail endemically ; Professor Eschricht, of Copenhagen, states that one-sixth of the inhabitants of Iceland are affected by these entozoa.

Hydatid tumours are usually developed very slowly ; their duration is almost always for several years, and it is not rare to meet with cases of which the earliest symptoms can be traced back for ten or fifteen years, or even longer.

When an hydatid tumour is situated in an organ which is essential to life, and which cannot be displaced and does not admit of distension, it may lead to the death of the patient before it has acquired a large size ; but when it is developed under other conditions, it has no immediate effect. In the latter case, it may continue for a long time without its being perceived, and may become of considerable dimensions before any marked functional derangement is evidenced, either because the viscera yield gradually to the pressure and are displaced, or because they become to some extent accustomed to the presence of the tumour, owing to its slow development.

When the tumour has attained to a certain size, varying according to the conditions of the individual case, and presses upon an organ through which the animal fluids or the alimentary substances pass, such as the urinary organs and the intestines, serious complications and even death may supervene, in consequence of the impediment which is presented to the natural course of the contents of these passages. If the healthy function of the organ which is affected is necessary to the existence of the patient, or if the function of this organ cannot be replaced by another, as happens with respect to the kidney, for example, the general health is disturbed, and the patient becomes weak and emaciated. Fever, diarrhœa, and colliquative sweats come on, and death occurs without its being possible to assign it to any other cause than to the destruction of a function which is necessary for the maintenance of life.

In other cases, which are undoubtedly more common, some intercurrent affection, pneumonia more often than any other, carries off the patient before the complications just enumerated have made sufficient progress to cause death.

The hydatid cyst is not painful, of itself; and it is not a rare thing to find, upon making post-mortem examinations of persons who have died from some other disease, cysts which had never been even suspected during the lifetime of the individuals.

When the cyst has arrived at a considerable size, it occasions a feeling of distension, of fulness, or of weight rather than of actual pain. This is not the case, however, when the neighbouring parts are attacked by inflammation or suppuration; pain, which is exacerbated by pressure or by motion, is then present, accompanied by rigors, fever, and all the symptoms and consequences of deep-seated suppuration.

The opening of the tumour into a large serous cavity gives rise to immediate and very severe inflammation; when the tumour opens into the vessels, it produces more or less grave disorders, in proportion to the size of the communication between the cyst and the vessels, and the quantity of matter which passes out of the former into the latter.

If the tumour opens into a mucous cavity, a means of elimination is afforded to the contents of the cyst, which is not unfrequently emptied gradually, and progresses towards a favourable termination without any bad symptoms.

The ordinary symptoms of hydatids are the existence of a tumour in some part of the body, the phenomena produced by the compression of one of the viscera situated in the same region as the swelling, and the evacuation, either through the natural passages or through an accidental opening, of vesicles or of some portions of the hydatids.

In the early stages of their development the diagnosis of hydatid tumours is generally very difficult, or even impossible; but, at a later period, the signs which admit of their being recognised become more evident.

There will be reason for the belief that a tumour is formed by hydatids when it has produced neither pain, nor fever, nor constitutional disturbance, although it has existed for a long time, and has been slowly developed until it has attained to a considerable bulk. It should also be borne in mind that the hydatid tumour is usually globular, smooth, and elastic; that it yields a dull sound upon percussion, and that fluctuation may often be perceived in it. Sometimes, too, it is the seat of a peculiar trembling sensation, which may be regarded as pathognomonic of hydatids.

When the hand is applied to a cyst containing acephalocysts, in such a manner as to hold it as firmly as possible, a trembling motion, analogous to that which is felt in any vibrating body, will be perceived if a sharp blow be given to the tumour with the other hand. If the tumour be situated where auscultation can be employed as well as percussion, a vibratory sound may be heard.

This phenomenon is not present in all cases of hydatid tumours, and its intensity varies according to the nature of the individual case. The observations of M. Briançon, who was the first to call attention to it, show that it is necessary that only a small quantity of fluid should be contained in the cyst, in order that the vibrations should be produced.[1]

It has been stated by some writers that the hydatid trembling is not present when the tumour contains only a single hydatid, but this opinion has been proved to be erroneous; it would probably

[1] " Essai sur le Diagnostic et le Traitement des Acéphalocystes," Paris, 1828.

never be observed after the tumour has become atheromatous.

When this phenomenon does exist, it decides the nature of the tumour, but we must be careful not to confound with it the crepitation which is sometimes produced in synovial bursæ, and in non-inflammatory abscesses which are subdivided by small partitions.

As a general rule, the absence of pain and of fever will prevent a hydatid tumour from being mistaken for an abscess, the absence of pulsation, and its slow development will distinguish it from an aneurism; and the absence of pain and of grave constitutional disturbance will suffice to establish a diagnosis between it and a cancerous tumour.

The diagnosis becomes more difficult when inflammation or suppuration have attacked the parts surrounding the cyst, as the pain, rigors, and fever might then induce the belief that it was an abscess, and the great disturbance of the system might cause it to be mistaken for a cancerous tumour; but the previous history of the case, and the fact of the tumour having reached a large size before the invasion of the fever and of the emaciation, which bears no resemblance to the cancerous cachexia, would throw some light upon the diagnosis, which the hydatid trembling, if present, would render complete.

The physical signs of hydatids, such as tumefaction, dulness on percussion, fluctuation, and the peculiar trembling cannot, in general, be perceived when the cyst is deeply situated in the chest or in the pelvis; and the diagnosis is usually impossible when the hydatid cyst is contained within the cavity of the cranium, as its bony parietes place an insuperable obstacle in the way of an examination.

In those cases in which the nature of a large-sized tumour has remained undetermined, the diagnosis may be settled by an exploratory puncture. A clear, limpid fluid extracted from the tumour, not coagulating upon the addition of acids or the application of heat, and leaving crystals of chloride of sodium after the evaporation of a few drops of the fluid placed upon a piece of glass, may generally be referred to hydatids. A turbid liquid, of a sero-purulent character, and which presents an atheromatous appearance when examined by the microscope, may also be considered as derived from hydatid tumours. Under either conditions, echinococci or their hooks are very frequently found in the fluid.

The exploratory puncture has been regarded by many writers as being dangerous when it passes through a serous cavity; but if it is made with a capillary trocar, the risk is really very small.

When the cyst has been ruptured, the expulsion of hydatid membranes either through the natural passages, or through an adventitious opening, renders the diagnosis perfect; but a simple ocular inspection is not always sufficient to decide whether the membranes which are expelled are those of hydatids. These fragments have a peculiar appearance; they are, as has already been stated, formed of very fine layers, arranged one upon another, which, when examined by the microscope, exhibit upon their transverse section parallel lines, somewhat similar to the leaves of a book.

The diagnosis may, at the same time, be confirmed

by the discovery of the hooks of echinococci; and there would also be additional reasons for the suspicion that the tumour belonged to the hydatid class if the matter which was expelled had the appearance of pus, and presented under the microscope the characteristics which have been already described as belonging to the contents of atheromatous cysts.

Hydatid tumours do not, of themselves, constitute a grave affection, as they do not usually produce any general derangement of the system, but they may be attended by serious results on account of their situation or large size.

The prognosis, being necessarily subordinate to the diagnosis, cannot be established in the earliest stages of the development of vesicular worms, nor when these entozoa exist in some part which is inaccessible to exploration. The cysts which are situated in the limbs, in the parietes of the body, and in other regions where surgical treatment can be readily employed, may usually be cured without much difficulty, and are not likely to prove fatal or dangerous to life. Hydatid tumours which, although they have lasted for a long period, do not show any further increase, or which even undergo an appreciable diminution of size, may be regarded as already tending to a favourable termination; and the same is also the case when a hydatid tumour has opened either externally, or into some viscus which possesses an external communication, and has not given rise to any marked complications, whilst it has diminished in size.

Hydatid tumours are, on the contrary, very serious when they occupy an important organ, when they have acquired a large bulk, when the walls of the cyst have become more or less cartilaginous or osseous, when the cysts are multiple, and when emaciation or inflammatory symptoms have followed their appearance.

They are commonly mortal if the general symptoms are persistent and become worse, after they have opened into some organ which possesses an external communication, if the matter which is expelled assumes a gangrenous character, if pneumonia or deep-seated suppuration supervene, or if the cyst has discharged its contents into a large serous cavity.

The pathological phenomena and the complications to which hydatids give rise, present, according to the situations in which the entozoa exist, certain points of difference which it is requisite to notice before the various methods of treatment are indicated.

CHAPTER XIX.

HYDATIDS WHICH ARE IN RELATION WITH THE CIRCULATORY SYSTEM.

HYDATIDS are sometimes observed in the blood-vessels, either as a result of their development there, which is a very doubtful point, or else as a result of their accidental communication with the vessels, through the perforation of the walls of the latter,— the vesicular worms having been primarily developed in the structure of the heart, or in some organ which does not form a part of the circulatory system.

Hydatids which are developed in the substance of the heart may acquire a considerable size before they give rise to any evident derangement in the functions of that organ ; in some cases, they do not produce any appreciable phenomena until the cyst is ruptured, and its contents are poured out into the cardiac cavities ; the vesicles, either whole or broken into pieces, are carried into the vessels with the blood, and present such obstacles to the due performance of the circulation as to produce immediate complications, and occasionally sudden death.

This latter termination, without any premonitory symptoms, has been known to occur when the hydatid cyst in the heart was unbroken.

There is no sign which can be considered as diagnostic of the existence of vesicular worms in the heart.

Hydatids which are developed in an organ which does not form a part of the circulatory system, may produce perforation of the blood-vessels with which the cyst is in relation ; the result of this perforation is the introduction of the fluid contained in the cyst, of atheromatous matter, and of the vesicles themselves or of their fragments, into the vessels.

The introduction of the contents of an hydatid cyst into the current of the circulation must necessarily lead to serious derangements, which are of varied intensity, in proportion to the size of the perforation, and to the quantity and condition of the fluid which is admixed with the blood.

The bile itself may, in cases of hydatids of the

liver, be effused into a cyst which is in relation at one part with the biliary canals, and at another part with the veins, and in this manner the blood may become indirectly charged with bile.

The cases which have been placed upon record are sufficient to show that the communication of a hydatid cyst with the veins may give rise to the phenomena of phlebitis, of purulent infection of the blood, of pneumonia, and perhaps also of pulmonary gangrene, and of different acute affections of various organs which are situated at a distance from the primary lesion, and which are secondarily affected as a result of the deterioration or poisoning of the blood.

According to Dr. Davaine, the communication of the blood-vessels with hydatid cysts is not of infrequent occurrence ; and the numerous interesting cases which he has collected tend to establish the correctness of his opinion.

CHAPTER XX.

HYDATIDS WHICH ARE IN RELATION WITH THE ORGANS OF RESPIRATION.

THE hydatids which are in relation with the respiratory organs are either developed within the thoracic cavity itself, or else are developed first within the abdomen, and afterwards invade the chest in consequence of their great increase in size.

Hydatids developed within the cavity of the thorax are not very common ; they usually exist in the pulmonary tissue. Those which are developed between the pleura and the ribs, or in the mediastina, are very rare ; and it would be impossible to determine their position during the lifetime of the patient, unless the tumours had acquired large proportions.

Hydatids of the lungs usually exist in the lower lobes, and especially upon the right side ; very few cases are recorded in which the cysts were developed in the upper or middle portions of the lungs.

It is a rare occurrence to find two cysts in the same lung, but the cases in which a cyst was present in each lung are more common. When hydatids exist in the chest, the liver is often similarly affected.

In the greater proportion of cases the intra-thoracic cyst contains a single hydatid which occupies its whole cavity. This cyst has thin, smooth walls, at any rate until it has undergone some changes of structure ; sometimes it is of enormous size, and fills up the whole of one side of the chest. The affected side is then notably enlarged, the intercostal spaces are deeper than in the normal state, and the lung, which is folded upon itself and flattened, or reduced to a thin layer, is pressed back towards its root, or the upper part of the chest, or against the vertebral column, and the heart, which is changed in position according to the side from which the pressure of the hydatid is exerted, may be forced either towards the left or the right axilla, or towards the epigastrium. The liver may also be displaced, and pushed lower down into the abdominal cavity.

When the cyst is large, or when it is situated close to the pleura, the cavity of the latter is generally destroyed, and the serous folds are united together by firm adhesions. In consequence of the obliteration of the cavity of the pleura, the cyst may find its way towards the surface, and open either through the thoracic or the abdominal parietes, or through the diaphragm.

The hydatids may also escape, through the perforation of the bronchi ; and the cyst may thus be emptied, and a cure effected.

The cavity which remains after the total expulsion of the hydatids is contracted and cicatrised ; it is usually single, and there does not commonly exist in it, as in tuberculous cavities, any tendency to the formation of new and analogous pathological products.

If the hydatid tumour is very large, or of long previous duration, it is only emptied gradually, on account either of the induration of its walls, or of the nature of its contents. The patient, becoming exhausted by the sympathetic fever, cough and expectoration, or by some intercurrent affection, probably dies before the pouch is completely closed.

Hydatids situated in the lungs may also open into the pleura or the pericardium, but this termination is exceedingly rare in consequence of the strong adhesions which usually take place between the folds of which those membranes are formed. Death invariably follows the discharge of the contents of the cyst into either of these cavities.

The duration of hydatid tumours developed in the respiratory organs is always considerable. In many of the cases which have been recorded, the existence of the tumours could be traced back for two or more years prior to the period at which the patient applied for medical advice, or before serious complications presented themselves. The average duration of these hydatids is from two to four years.

Persons who are affected with hydatid cysts in the cavity of the thorax do not experience any functional derangement until the tumours have attained to a large size ; and, until the later stages of the disorder, the digestion, secretions, and pulse continue natural, and there are no febrile symptoms, although the sleep is disturbed, in consequence of the embarrassment to the respiration. Pains, which are acute, persistent, and subject to exacerbation, are often felt in the side, or in the back, or at the epigastrium. The patient lays upon the back, or upon the affected side.

The most constant, and the most marked, symptom is the difficulty of breathing, of which there are frequent paroxysms, sometimes almost amounting to suffocation ; there is also a dry cough, or only slight expectoration. When the cyst has established a communication with the bronchial tubes, the cough is severe, and the expectoration becomes more abundant. The matter which is expectorated is a serous, puriform, or atheromatous fluid, containing fragments of hydatids ; it may be either inodorous or fetid, or may even have a gangrenous odour, according to the state of the cyst, or of the part of the lung in which the cyst is situated. The expectoration is occasionally tinged with blood ; and, in some instances, the hœmoptysis is very considerable.

The hydatids which are expectorated whole are generally small, or they may be expelled in fragments of variable size, collected into a little ball ; echinococci, or their hooks, can sometimes be detected amongst these fragments.   The expectoration of the contents of the cyst recurs at irregular intervals, usually of several days, and sometimes of several weeks ; when they are discharged in large quantity, urgent symptoms of suffocation, which may even endanger the life of the patient, supervene.

The extent of the time which is requisite for the expulsion of hydatids from the lungs varies in proportion to the size of the cyst, and probably also according to the consistence of its walls ; the expulsion of the hydatids may occupy a period of many months.

The physical signs of hydatid tumours of the lungs are evidenced in a ratio to their volume, number, and situation.   An enlargement of one or both sides of the chest, and of the intercostal spaces, may be observed, together with displacement of the heart or of the liver, dulness upon percussion over a certain extent of the chest, and absence of the respiratory murmur, upon auscultation.   The chest is partially deformed, in a manner which is not usual in pleuritic effusion ; and fluctuation may be perceived when the cyst becomes superficial.

Hydatids of the organs of respiration have been seldom detected unless when they have had some external communication ; and in the majority of the cases which have been recorded, the symptoms were supposed to be due to pleuritic effusion.   The long duration of the disorder, the signs of extensive effusion without any very marked constitutional disturbance, and without fever, the peculiar deformity of the chest, and the great displacement of the heart or of the liver, may induce a suspicion of the real affection. The total absence of the respiratory murmur, accompanied by dulness upon percussion, will also aid in the diagnosis, which may be confirmed, in the majority of cases, by an exploratory puncture. This operation is not attended with much risk, as the adhesions between the two folds of the pleura usually obliterate its cavity.

In those cases in which hydatids or echinococci are expectorated, the diagnosis is generally easy, as it is only necessary to ascertain the nature of the expectorated matter. A careful examination into the facts connected with the individual case will decide whether the entozoa are situated in the lungs or in the liver.

Hydatid cysts which have been developed in any of the abdominal viscera, and especially in the upper portion of the liver, may force up the diaphragm, press upon the lungs, and thus produce an impediment to their free expansion. Like the hydatids which have been developed within the thoracic cavity itself, they may perforate, and discharge their contents into, the pleura or the pericardium, or they may establish a communication with one of the bronchi, and empty themselves externally through this passage. The symptoms, progress, and termination of these cases present a considerable analogy to those of hydatid cysts which are primarily situated within the chest.

The hydatids which are developed near the upper

surface of the liver press forcibly against the diaphragm, and, indirectly, against the lungs ; the liver
also extends lower down than in the healthy condition, and may even be felt below the borders of the
false ribs.　The lung may be pushed up as high as
the third, or even the second, rib, without perforation
of the diaphragm ; great dyspnœa, and several of the
physical signs of effusion into the pleura result from
this abnormal condition, and their constant occurrence accounts for the fact that the majority of such
cases have been mistaken, during the life-time of the
patient for hydrothorax or pleurisy.[1]

The diagnosis of these tumours must always be
very uncertain, but it may be sometimes possible to
distinguish them when symptoms have been observed
similar to those which are produced by hydatids
situated in the pleura, or at the base of the right
lung, and when, in addition, the liver extends lower
than usual.　In some cases, also, fluctuation or even
hydatid-trembling may be felt below the edges of the
inferior ribs, so that the nature of the affection would
then be no longer doubtful.

Cysts which are developed in the part of the
liver which is nearest to the lungs occasionally perforate the diaphragm, either by their pressure, or as
the result of some violent effort of the patient, and

---

[1] As an illustration of the displacement of the thoracic
viscera which results from the presence of hydatids in the left
hypochondrium, a case may be referred to, in which, owing to the
development of a cyst in the spleen, the heart was pushed up as
high as the third rib, and the lung, which was scarcely larger
than the closed hand, was pressed towards the roots of the
bronchi; the diaphragm, which was considerably raised, was not
perforated.

their contents then escape into the pleura. Acute pain in the side commonly indicates this accident, and is accompanied by a severe and rapidly mortal attack of pleurisy, owing to the inflammation which at once sets in ; in some instances, however, the progress of the malady is less rapid, and a communication may be established between the pleura and the bronchi, when the signs of pneumothorax will succeed to those of pleuritic effusion.

An accurate diagnosis of such a complication could scarcely be formed, unless the existence of a hydatid cyst in one of the abdominal viscera had been previously ascertained.

The cases which have been recorded of cysts of the liver opening into the pleura are much more numerous than those of cysts situated in the lungs which have opened into the same cavity ; this greater relative frequency is doubtless due to the fact that intra-thoracic hydatids generally cause adhesions between the two layers of serous membrane, and also, in a smaller degree, to the circumstance of hydatids being more frequent in the liver than in the lungs.

When hepatic cysts have formed a communication with the bronchi, the contents of the cyst may be expectorated, and the pouch emptied similarly to the termination which is observed when cysts developed in the lungs open into those passages ; if a means of elimination is thus procured, some hopes of a recovery may be entertained.

The course and symptoms of such cases are very similar to those which are present when intra-thoracic cysts open into the bronchi; sometimes a considerable enlargement of the liver may be observed, and in a few cases bile has been known to be mixed with the expectorated matter.

Chapter XXI.

HYDATIDS DEVELOPED IN THE ABDOMINAL VISCERA.

HYDATIDS have never been found free within the peritoneum, unless they had been previously developed in a cyst which, after its rupture, had discharged its contents into the peritoneal cavity. The hydatids which exist in the abdomen are developed in the substance of one of the abdominal viscera, or else in the sub-serous areolar tissue ; in the latter situation, the cysts are frequently multiple ; hydatids are more common in the liver than elsewhere.

As a rule, these hydatid tumours pass through all their stages of growth in the part where they are primarily developed ; but, sometimes, either as a result of accident, or in consequence of its large size, the cyst is ruptured, and its contents are discharged into some other viscus, or else externally, owing to the perforation of the abdominal parietes.

The general observations which have been made upon hydatids in a former chapter are especially applicable to vesicular worms in the liver, and it will therefore only be necessary to point out certain peculiarities which depend upon the structure, function, position, and relations of that organ.

Sometimes only a single hydatid cyst exists in the hepatic substance, but frequently two or three, and occasionally five or six, or even more, may be found ; at the same time, hydatids may be met with in other viscera, and, generally speaking, when hydatids exist elsewhere, the liver will also be found to be attacked by these entozoa.

The hydatids of this organ are very slowly developed ; if they are single, they seldom give rise to any functional disorder until they have acquired a large bulk. Digestion and nutrition are accomplished in a normal manner ; there is no pain, or if any exist it is of a vague nature, and consists rather in a sensation of weight and of distention than of actual suffering. These sensations occupy the epigastric region, the right hypochondrium, and sometimes the right shoulder.

When the cyst has attained to considerable dimensions, the liver becomes atrophied. If no special complications supervene, emaciation and constitutional disturbance are now present, and the patient finally succumbs to the effects of the wasting, which can only be attributed to the destruction of the secretory function of the liver.

It seldom happens that a single cyst induces complete atrophy, as that part of the organ which escapes compression may suffice for the maintenance of the hepatic functions. When several cysts attack the liver, the systemic wasting is more certain and more rapid, and serious complications, such as erysipelas, pneumonia, pleurisy, and peritonitis, frequently occur, in consequence of the debilitated condition of the patient. In several cases, a strong predisposition to gangrene, or to hœmorrhage, has been observed in various parts of the body.

Hydatids of the liver do not very often produce jaundice, and when this phenomenon occurs it is usually due to one of three conditions, viz., more or less extensive inflammation of the substance of the liver, obstruction of the biliary passages by the vesicular worms, or the compression of the tumour upon the ductus communis choledochus, or one of the larger branches of the hepatic duct. It is probable that jaundice would also come on if the biliary ducts and the veins communicated with the cyst, as the bile might thus find its way into the veins, and into the circulation.

If the tumour presses upon the principal venous trunks which are in relation with the liver, œdema of the lower extremities, or even serous effusion into the peritoneal cavity, may result from the impediment to the circulation.

The presence of an hydatid cyst sometimes gives rise to acute inflammation of the hepatic tissue, terminating in suppuration ; this inflammatory action is produced either by the rapid growth of the cyst, or by its having attained to a large size. It may also occur in consequence of external injury, such as blows, or after operations performed for the purpose of evacuating the cyst.

It is extremely difficult to correctly diagnose a small hydatid cyst in the liver ; but when it is of · large size, the existence in the right hypochondrium of a well-marked, smooth tumour, which has grown gradually, and is unattended by much pain, by fever, or by jaundice, can scarcely be attributed to any other cause than hydatids. When the cyst is developed near the upper border of the liver, it pushes up the diaphragm, and may be distinguished from pleuritic effusion by the signs which have been already described.

An hydatid tumour of the liver is readily distinguishable from an abscess in the same situation, as the latter seldom acquires a large volume without being preceded or accompanied by pain or fever, and it may also be distinguished from a cancerous tumour of the liver by its larger size, and by its forming a globular, smooth swelling, whilst in cancer the enlargement usually presents a nodulated character, besides which the various symptoms of cancerous cachexia will generally complete the diagnosis.

Distension of the gall-bladder may more probably be mistaken for an hydatid cyst; it is, in fact, globular, smooth, and compressible, but it is constantly, and almost from the commencement of the affection, accompanied by great yellowness of the skin, and by acute pain, and the hydatid-trembling can never be detected in it.

Hydatids of the liver may also be mistaken for aneurism of the aorta, which, like an hydatid cyst, is globular, and painless upon pressure, and does not give rise to jaundice, or to serous effusion into the peritoneum, or to disordered digestion, or to impediment to the respiration, at least not until it has acquired considerable dimensions; but the very distinct pulsations, and the bellows-sound which is perceptible upon applying the stethoscope at the level of the last dorsal, or of the first lumbar, vertebra, are usually characteristic symptoms of aneurismal tumours in this region.

Notwithstanding these signs, which are sufficiently distinctive in many cases, there are some cases in which the diagnosis presents the greatest difficulties. These difficulties especially arise when the growth of the tumour has been more rapid than is usual, when it is accompanied by pain and febrile symptoms, when some peculiar circumstances, such as external violence, have modified its progress, when by the pressure exercised upon the biliary ducts, the portal vein, or the vena cava, the tumour has produced either jaundice, ascites, or œdema of the lower extremities, or when several cysts give an uneven character to the enlargement in the hypochondrium ; but in all of these cases, if the hydatid-trembling should be absent, an exploratory puncture with a capillary trocar, when it can be resorted to without danger, would decide whether the affection proceeded from hydatids, or not.

Hydatids are much less common in the spleen than in the liver ; and they generally co-exist with a similar disease in the latter organ, or in some other region of the abdomen. They are usually developed in the sub-peritoneal areolar tissue, or in the vicinity of the spleen, and only invade the spleen subsequently, although they may also originate in the interior of the substance of that organ. They have thinner walls than those which are situated in the liver ; and the surrounding substance often remains healthy. The mode of their development, the size to which they attain, and the changes which they undergo, do not present any special characteristics.

Their pathological phenomena are analogous to those produced by cysts in the liver, with the exception only that the symptoms dependent upon the compression or ulceration of the biliary passages are absent, when the former viscus is concerned ; like the corresponding cysts in the liver, hydatids of the spleen displace the neighbouring viscera, invade the thoracic cavity, and give rise to similar complications.

The diagnostic signs of hydatids in the spleen differ only slightly from those of hepatic hydatids,— the principal points of distinction being as regards the side which is affected, and the absence of biliary derangement when the spleen alone is affected.

Hydatids may also be developed in other viscera, or in other regions, of the abdomen. They may be found in some part of the great visceral cavity, not within the peritoneum, but in the areolar tissue, external to that membrane ; they may originate from the internal surface of the abdominal parietes, or from the external surface of the intestines, of the bladder, or some other organ, or in the substance of the omenta or of the mesentery.

The cyst is invested externally by the peritoneum, which forms a more or less complete envelope for it, and it is sometimes detached from the position whence it originally commenced its growth, and is then only kept in position by a small peduncle. Hydatid tumours are more frequently multiple in these situations, perhaps, than in any other parts of the body. They acquire a very large size separately, or by their union may form a considerable mass.

When these cysts have attained to sufficient magnitude, they can be felt through the abdominal parietes ; they might then be mistaken for cancerous tumours, or for enlarged mesenteric glands, but, unlike these, they do not, for a long period, occasion either pain, functional derangements, or constitutional disturbance.

If they do not eventually, either through an accidental complication or as a result of their position, give rise to an acute and mortal affection of some adjacent organ, they always terminate by the production of such serious functional disorder that the patient becomes emaciated, falls into a decline, and dies.

Hydatid cysts of the liver, or of the other abdominal viscera, not infrequently open into the neighbouring serous or mucous cavities, in consequence either of external violence, or of some excessive effort on the part of the patient, or of great distension of the cyst.

When an hydatid cyst opens into a large serous cavity, the immediate inflammation which follows progresses very rapidly, and always leads to the death of the patient. This accident has been known to destroy life in a few hours, whilst, in other cases, death did not occur for several days ; the difference in the course of the affection may be accounted for by the relative size of the perforation, and the quantity and nature of the fluid which is effused.

The sudden subsidence of an abdominal tumour, sometimes preceded or accompanied by a sensation of internal rupture, the coincidence of violent pain, and the signs of peritonitis or of pleurisy, would admit of the supposition that the tumour had opened into the serous cavity of the abdomen or of the chest.

When a hydatid cyst opens into a cavity invested by mucous membrane, the hydatids are expelled, either whole or in fragments, by expectoration, or by vomiting, or with the evacuations, or the urine. In the present place we need only consider those cases in which the hydatids, having penetrated the alimentary canal, are discharged by vomiting or with the evacuations.

The opening of communication which is formed between the hydatid cyst and the intestines is generally very narrow, and permits only of the very slow discharge of the vesicles, so that their expulsion from the body occupies a considerable period, sometimes extending over several months. The perforation is not always sufficiently large to allow of the complete emptying of the cyst, which may then open into some other viscus, or at the surface of the body.

The passage of the contents of the cyst into the alimentary canal does not give rise to inflammation of the mucous membrane, and the only effect produced by it is usually diarrhœa, which is sometimes very difficult to control.

The opening of a cyst into the intestines may be known by the sensation of internal rupture which the patient often experiences, by the rapid subsidence of the tumour, and by the expulsion through one of the outlets of the body of vesicles, which are either whole or in fragments, and are recognisable by the naked eye or with the aid of the microscope, and which sometimes contain the hooklets of the echinococci.

This accident usually brings on a favourable termination of the affection.

Hydatids situated in the abdominal viscera sometimes open spontaneously through the parietes of the abdomen ; the vesicles and the matter contained in the cyst are discharged through the external aperture, and complete recovery may result. In other cases the fistula closes and is subsequently reopened, or the tumour establishes a new communication with the intestines.

CHAPTER XXII.

HYDATIDS SITUATED IN THE TRUE PELVIS.

ALTHOUGH the yielding nature of the parietes of the abdomen, and the ready displacement of the viscera contained within it, allow hydatids to grow to a large size without the production of any complications, the same is not the case when hydatids are developed in the true pelvis ; the resisting character of its walls, which prevent the displacement of the viscera, gives rise to compression of the pelvic organs, and, as soon as the tumour has acquired a moderate size, to very serious affections.

The hydatids in the pelvic cavity are usually developed in the areolar tissue which invests the various viscera. In the male they have no other primitive seat ; but in the female a cyst which has been developed in the ovary may extend into the recto-vesical pouch, and produce the same effects as if it had been developed in that situation.

The cysts of the true pelvis frequently form extensive and firm adhesions to the neighbouring viscera ; they compress the rectum, the bladder, and the vagina, and they force the uterus and the bladder either above or below their normal position, whilst they also flatten or alter the shape of these two organs by pressing them against the pubis, or some other portion of the hard walls of the pelvis.

Hydatid tumours often prevent the discharge of the urine, by compression or displacement of the bladder, or by the compression of the prostrate gland, or of the urethra ; catheterism is sometimes impossible, and the retention of the urine is complete.

The compression which these tumours exercise upon the rectum soon occasions constipation, and at a later period of the affection the passage of fœcal matter is totally prevented.   This obstacle to the passage of the fœces causes hypertrophy of the muscular fibres of the intestine above the seat of the obstruction.   A similar result has been observed in the bladder, and in the ureters.

A hydatid cyst in the pelvis, like a similar tumour in any other region of the body, may occasion ulceration of the neighbouring viscera, and be thus brought into communication with their cavities.   It may open into the bladder, or into the rectum, and be completely emptied ; recovery occasionally follows the discharge of the hydatid contents.   No case is recorded in which a hydatid cyst has spontaneously opened into the vagina, or the uterus ; the rigidity of the walls of the latter organ sufficiently explain this so far as the uterus is concerned. It is also very rare, owing to the nature of the walls of the pelvis, for a hydatid cyst to open externally.

The relative depth at which the cyst is situated is the principal circumstance which modifies the severity and time of appearance of the complications produced by its growth ; and the extent of the adhesions which it forms, and which prevent its rising towards the abdominal cavity, is also not without some influence upon the symptoms.

Hydatids in the pelvis could scarcely be mistaken for abscess in that region ; they might more readily be confounded, in the female, with a sanguineous tumour, but the formation of the latter is ordinarily accompanied by general indisposition, by menstrual derangements, and by pains, which is increased upon pressure, in the lower part of the abdomen.

Fibrous and cancerous tumours may be distinguished by their consistence, from hydatids, and, in the case of cancerous tumours, by the peculiar cachexia also.

In the majority of cases, an exploratory puncture will be necessary to establish the diagnosis ; the discharge of the hydatid liquid, and of the hooklets of the echinococci, or of some portion of the vesicular worm, would, of course, at once decide the character of the affection.

When the cyst has reached a large size, it may cause a projection above the pubis, and be recognised by means of palpation and percussion ; and, at the same time, a rectal or vaginal examination may lead to the discovery of a smooth, round, and painless tumour in the pelvic cavity.

CHAPTER XXIII.

HYDATIDS IN THE URINARY ORGANS.

HYDATIDS in the kidneys are rare; and only one of these organs is usually affected, in the same individual. The cyst is generally single, and the hydatids contained within its cavity are almost always multiple. The walls of the cyst are firm and fibrous, and sometimes even fibro-cartilaginous, or cretaceous; and its contents undergo various alterations of structure at different periods of their existence. The hydatid pouch may, in an advanced stage, be occasionally arrested in its growth, and its volume may even become so much contracted as to lead to a cure; but, more frequently, it continues to increase in size, and forms a considerable tumour, which produces general or partial distension of the kidney, and more or less complete atrophy of the substance of that organ. The part of the kidney which is occupied by a large-sized hydatid cyst, sometimes assumes a yellowish tint; and the pelvis of the kidney is, at the same time, connected with the cyst by means of organised false membrane, which is traversed by numerous vessels.

A section of the tumour usually exhibits the following arrangement: externally, it is formed by the atrophied and anœmic renal substance, which is still distinct in some parts, whilst in others it is reduced to simple areolar tissue, which is infiltrated with yellowish matter; in the interior, it is seen to be formed by a cyst which possesses strong walls, and is roughened, and of a yellowish colour upon its internal surface.

Hydatid cysts of the kidney may exist for a long time without producing any organic lesions, but they almost invariably terminate by the production of inflammation and ulceration of the surrounding parts, which are finally perforated; sometimes they open at the surface of the body, in the lumbar region, and sometimes they form a communication with the intestine; they also occasionally penetrate the cavity of the chest, and open into the bronchi. According to the situation at which the cyst opens, the hydatids are discharged through a lumbar fistula, or are expelled with the evacuations, or are expectorated during the fits of coughing.

More often, however, hydatid cysts of the kidney contract adhesions with the walls of the pelvis of the kidney, and open into its cavity. The smallest hydatids, and pieces of the larger ones, together with some of the serous or sero-purulent fluid contained in the cyst, are then passed with the urine. When this termination occurs, there is pain in the renal region, and sometimes retention of urine, caused by the obstruction which results from the entanglement of the hydatids in the pelvis of the kidney, in the ureter, or the urethra; the ureter becomes, after a time, considerably dilated.

The hydatid cysts in the kidney which are still unbroken do not ordinarily give rise to any complications or to any inconvenience, beyond that which is attributable to their bulk. When they have opened into the calices, or into the pelvis of the kidney, the hydatids which escape into the ureter, temporarily obstruct it, as has just been stated, and produce the symptoms which are common to all foreign bodies obstructing this passage, namely, difficult micturition, spasmodic pain in the ureter and kidney, hiccough, nausea, and vomiting ; sometimes the hydatids completely block up the urethra, and cause retention of urine, and acute pains in the bladder and urethra, which cease soon after the expulsion of the hydatids with the urine.

Hydatid cysts, developed in the kidney or in its immediate vicinity, form, whilst entire, a tumour which resembles that of chronic pyelitis, or of dropsy of the kidney; hydatid trembling, if it existed, would, however, serve to distinguish between them. It is not always easy to ascertain whether the cysts belong to the kidney or to the liver. The position of the cysts developed in the latter organ is usually more in front, and at the acute margin of the liver ; in some cases, the previous existence of an attack of jaundice or of functional derangement of the kidneys, may assist in clearing up the diagnosis.

The passage of hydatids with the urine determines the nature of the lumbar swelling, and it also indicates that the tumour does not belong to the liver ; but it is nevertheless necessary to bear in mind that hydatids which are expelled with the urine may come from a cyst situated in some other organ than the kidney.

If we may form an opinion from the progress of the affection, in the majority of the cases of cysts of the kidney which have been recorded, the prognosis of this species of tumour would be generally less

grave than that of renal tumours formed as a consequence of pyelitis. The hydatid cysts of the
kidney have, like those which are developed in other
organs, a great tendency to perforation, and to contraction after they have been completely emptied of
their contents ; so that the cases of recovery after
the evacuation of the hydatids through the urinary
passages, are not very rare, but it cannot be previously determined, in any given case, whether such a
complete discharge of the contents of the cyst will
take place, or not.

Chapter XXIV.

HYDATIDS SITUATED IN THE SUPERFICIAL PARTS OF THE BODY AND IN THE BONES.

HYDATIDS are very seldom developed in the superficial parts of the body, and more rarely still in the
extremities ; they are equally infrequent in the
organs which are placed superficially, such as those
of the face, and the external organs of generation.

Dr. Davaine gives an account of about forty cases
which he has collected from various sources. Of
these, eight occurred in the orbit, one in the lachrymal
gland, and one in the eyelid ; two cases are recorded
of hydatid cysts in the canine fossa, one in the lower
jaw, and one in the tonsil ; seven cases, of which
three appear to have been connected with the thyroid
gland, were observed in different parts of the neck ;
thirteen occurred in the parietes of the body, and

nine in the extremities, of which only two were situated in the upper, and the remaining seven in the lower, limbs.

It is doubtful whether some of these cases may be looked upon as having been really due to hydatids, or whether they were only cysticerci or serous cysts, especially those cases which occurred in the eye, or its appendages.

The symptoms which are produced by hydatids in the situations which have been mentioned, are similar to those which are present when other tumours exist in the same situations.

Nineteen cases have been collected by Dr. Davaine, of hydatids developed in the osseous system ; both the long and flat bones have been known to be affected. The following is a list of the various bones in which hydatids have been observed, and of the number of cases which have occurred in each bone :— In the tibia six cases; in the humerus, femur, frontal bone, and pelvis, two cases each ; and one case each in the temporal bone, sphenoid bone, and a phalanx of the index finger.

Generally speaking, the hydatids occupy the diploe in the flat bones, and the spongy portion in the long bones ; they have, however, been known to be developed in the shafts of the long bones, and to invade the whole extent of the medullary cavity. Sometimes the hydatids occupy distinct cells in the spongy tissue, but they are more frequently enclosed in a single pouch. The development of this pouch is very slow, and, in the majority of cases, its duration has extended over several years. It may acquire the dimensions of the closed hand.

It is smooth upon its internal surface, at least in its earliest stages, and consists of a delicate membrane, which is distinct from the surrounding bony tissue; upon the bony tissue may be observed digital depressions, which are caused by the pressure of the hydatids, and are analogous in their appearance to the little depressions which are seen on the internal surface of the cranium.

The cyst undergoes modifications in form which bear a relation to the obstacles which are opposed to its growth in various directions; and it also undergoes modifications of structure which are similar to those observed in hydatid cysts in other parts of the body. The bony walls which enclose it acquire, at first, an increase in size proportional to that of the hydatid pouch; they are distended, and become thinner, so that the portion of the bone in which the hydatids are contained forms a swelling of uniform dimensions; at a later period, those portions of the bone which are thinnest are absorbed, and the cyst comes into contact with the soft parts which it encroaches upon as its development continues, and finally the neighbouring organs are seriously affected, owing to their compression or displacement.

The hydatids which are situated in the cranial bones give rise to the same complications as are produced by cystic tumours developed in the brain; hydatids contained in the walls of the orbit cause protrusion of the eyeball, and loss of vision; and those which are developed in the long bones may eventually invade an articular cavity and produce severe arthritis.

Hydatids in bones are usually painless at the

commencement, although in some cases the patient may complain of a fixed, deep-seated sensation of uneasiness at an early period of the affection. A smooth, uniform tumour, of a bony consistence, makes its appearance at the diseased part ; it increases gradually and regularly in size ; it subsequently becomes soft at various points, and fluctuation, together with a hard, osseous border around the softened portion, may sometimes be felt. If the tumour be deeply situated, and surrounded by a dense covering of muscles, it may remain undiscovered for a considerable length of time ; and the bone becomes so thinned and brittle, in consequence of the gradual absorption, that, during a muscular effort, it is suddenly broken.

When the cyst is opened, either spontaneously, or by a bistoury, or by any other means, the hydatids are liberated, and inflammation and suppuration are produced. General complications, which are usually of a serious nature, then supervene ; the suppuration lasts for a long period, because the rigidity of the bony tissue prevents the contraction of the cyst ; and the constitution of the patient is thus gradually undermined, so that the case often terminates fatally.

CHAPTER XXV.

THE MEDICAL AND SURGICAL TREATMENT OF HYDATID TUMOURS.

THE efficacy of the various plans of medical treatment which have been adopted in the case of hydatids is very uncertain; but further trial is necessary before we ought to condemn, as useless, the different remedial agents which have been suggested by different observers.

With regard to prophylactic treatment nothing can be regarded as satisfactory until our knowledge of the mode of transmission of hydatids, and of the circumstances which favour their development in the human body, is more certain than it is at present.

Upon a consideration of the nature, and of the situation of hydatids, it is evident that the remedies which ought to be administered for their destruction are such as are soluble in the animal fluids, and which might, by their solution and absorption, get into the circulation, and thus be brought into contact with the hydatid cyst, into which they might penetrate by endosmosis; it is also requisite that these medicinal substances should act poisonously upon the hydatids, but not upon the human organs.

Baumes has published several cases which tend to show that calomel possesses some efficacy against hydatids; but several other authors state that they have employed this remedy unsuccessfully in cases where the existence of hydatids was proved by post-mortem examination, and that even when the administration of the mercury was pushed so far as to produce salivation, the progress of the affection did not appear to undergo any modification.

The chloride of sodium has been recommended, in consequence of the joint fact that sheep fed in meadows which are impregnated with salt, are free from hydatids, and that the same animals, although they are affected with hydatids through their having been kept in marshy places, may be cured by removal into meadows where a certain proportion of salt can be taken with their food. Laennec states that he has used saline baths with much advantage in the treatment of hydatids. Dr. Davaine observes, however, that as chloride of sodium naturally exists in the liquid of hydatids in considerable quantity, it is consequently not very probable that this salt can occasion the death of the vesicular worms. If it favour the cure, it does so doubtless by acting upon the system of the patient, as perhaps it does upon the constitution of sailors in protecting them from hydatids; but the absence of hydatids in sailors, and in animals which graze in meadows which are impregnated with common salt, may be due to circumstances which prevent the transmission of these entozoa.

The iodide of potassium has been employed in the treatment of hydatids, but its efficacy has not been more fully proved than that of the chloride of sodium.

The use of the iodide of potassium internally might be seconded by the inunction of iodine ointment over the seat of the tumour.

Sulphuretted baths might be tried, with advantage in some cases. The medical treatment of hydatids is of more certain value when the tumour produces various complications, such as the inflammation and suppuration of adjacent organs ; and blood-letting, leeches, baths, and cataplasms may then be usefully employed, according to the nature of the individual case. Under special circumstances some internal remedies may also be resorted to ; such as narcotics to allay the paroxysms of coughing which are caused by the passage of the contents of the cyst into the bronchi, and turpentine when a cyst developed in the kidney has opened into the pelvis of the kidney.

Electricity has been suggested for the purpose of destroying hydatids, and in one case, of which the particulars were communicated by Guérault to the Société de Chirurgie of Paris, this method was successful. In this case, Dr. Thorarensen, of Iceland, introduced long, fine steel needles into the tumour, at its two opposite extremities, and through these he transmitted a series of electric shocks. The cure was prompt and complete ; the tumour gradually subsided, and the hydatids, which were probably absorbed, did not make any re-appearance.[1]

Cold applied over the hydatid tumour during a sufficiently long period to admit of its penetrating the mass, might perhaps destroy the echinococci or the vesicle which encloses them, and in this manner prevent the further growth of the tumour, or promote

[1] Note sur la maladie hydatique du fois en Islande, et l'emploi de l'electro-puncture à la destruction des Acéphalocystes.—*Gazette des Hôpitaux*, 1857.

its absorption. This plan is worthy of a trial in those cases in which the application of the frigorific mixture would not be attended with inconvenience or with danger to the organs situated in the vicinity of the cyst; Dr. Arnott's mode of producing cold is the best which could be adopted.

The surgical operations which have been proposed, and practised, in the treatment of hydatid tumours may be arranged into three classes :—

1. Those which procure the evacuation of the contents of the cyst;

2. Those which procure the modification, or the absorption of the matters contained within the tumour;

3. Those which have for their object the extirpation of the cyst.

The evacuation of the contents of the tumour is accomplished in various ways; these are the single puncture, repeated punctures, puncture with the formation of a permanent opening, simple incision, repeated incisions, and the application of some caustic.

Simple puncture has been performed with a view either to enable the practitioner to ascertain the nature of the tumour, or to bring about its cure. The exploratory value of this method has been already described, so that only its advantages and its drawbacks need now be discussed.

When the trocar does not have to pass through any important organ, or any serous cavity, in order to reach the cyst, the operation will be harmless; but when it must traverse a large serous cavity, a puncture, even although made with a capillary trocar, may give rise to serious, or sometimes mortal, complications, owing to the escape of the hydatid fluid into the cavity.

M. Boinet has pointed out certain precautions, by the adoption of which the escape of the hydatid liquid into the abdominal cavity may be prevented. When the canula is withdrawn from the cyst through the opening in the abdominal parietes the fingers of the left hand should be very carefully applied at the spot where the trocar has been inserted, so as to press the abdominal parietes against the cyst, and to keep it so closely in apposition with the tumour that, when the canula is withdrawn from the cyst, no interspace is left between it and the abdominal parietes. These precautions having been properly taken, the canula is to be withdrawn, and the pressure is to be kept up during a few minutes after its withdrawal, so that the small opening made by the introduction of the trocar into the cyst may be completely obliterated, and the escape of fluid into the peritoneum be prevented; the cyst is then to be lightly compressed by means of graduated compresses and of a bandage passed round the body. The patient should be directed to remain in the recumbent posture during thirty-six or forty-eight hours after the operation.[1]

When it is necessary for the puncture to pass through a large serous cavity, it has been recommended by M. Jobert to leave the canula fixed in the opening for twenty-four hours. In this manner

[1] "Traitement des tumeurs hydatiques du foie par les ponctions capillaires et par les ponctions suivies d'injections iodées," by M. Boinet. Paris, 1859.

adhesive inflammation of the serous membrane is produced, and the effusion of the matter contained within the cyst into the peritoneal cavity is prevented.

The method of treatment by repeated punctures, which has been equally successful with the plan just described, has for its object the gradual diminution of the size of the tumour, so that the cyst may have sufficient time to contract upon itself, and that the neighbouring viscera may gradually resume their normal position.

Incision has been resorted to principally when the hydatid tumour, forming a projection at the surface of the body, has threatened to burst, or when, in consequence of an error in diagnosis, the character of the tumour has been mistaken.

In a large proportion of the cases in which this operation has been performed, the termination of the affection has proved successful ; but it should be observed that in the majority of these cases it was not requisite for the incision to traverse any serous cavity in order to reach the cyst, or else that the adhesions established between the tumour and the adjacent parts had formed a secure protection against the escape of the contents of the cyst into the pleura or the peritoneum.

The operation of incision at two distinct periods has only been practised upon a few occasions. Its object is to prevent the contents of a cyst situated in the liver from passing into the peritoneum ; the first incision is made to extend as far as the peritoneum, and the bottom of the wound is plugged with a piece of lint ; after an interval of a few days, when adhesions of the peritoneal surfaces are supposed to be fully established, a second is made, extending into the hydatid tumour, and the cyst is emptied.

The method of opening hydatid tumours by the application of caustic has been known for a long time, but it was only resorted to for the purpose of evacuating the hydatid contents. Another more important object may, however, be attained, namely, the opening of a cyst situated in an internal organ without the risk of effusion into the neighbouring serous cavity. This operation is especially suitable for the treatment of hydatids in the liver.

The caustic is applied repeatedly at intervals of a few days, in order that the adhesions produced by the inflammatory action which is set up may effectually prevent the escape of the cystic contents into the peritoneum; if the eschars, upon their removal, do not lay open the cavity of the cyst, the aperture may be completed by means of incision or puncture.

The agents employed in this operation are caustic potash, or the Vienna paste, which is a compound of caustic potash with quicklime.

Dr. Davaine gives the details of twelve cases, in which this plan was the only one adopted; in six of these a cure was effected; in one the termination of the case was not learnt, but as the tumour rapidly diminished in size, and as no immediate bad results followed, the patient most probably recovered; in the other five cases death occurred at a variable period, ranging from a few weeks to a few months after the performance of the operation. An examination into these five cases of failure shows that in one there were nervous complications altogether independent of

the method of treatment ; in another the unsuc-
cessful termination of the case arose from insufficient
attention to the dressing of the wound subsequently
to the evacuation of the cyst ; and in two more the
cysts existed in such numbers that every other mode
of treatment would have most likely been attended
with a similar result.

The chief objections which have been urged
against the plan of treatment by caustic are :—
1. That it acts slowly ; 2. That its effects are occasionally difficult to control ; 3. That it may cause
peritonitis ; and 4. That it does not always produce
adhesion.

The first objection, which would have some weight
when a simple abscess is concerned, is not of any
value as regards hydatid tumours ; besides which,
the opening of the tumour may be accelerated by the
more frequent application of the caustic. In one
case, quoted by Davaine, the cyst was opened after
four applications of the caustic, extending over a
space of only seven days ; and in another instance
the cyst was opened on the seventh day, after the
application of the caustic at short intervals ; in this
second case more than six pints of purulent matter
and of hydatids were discharged upon the removal of
the eschar, and a marked improvement soon took
place in the health of the patient, who ultimately
recovered.

The second objection does not hold good as regards
the Vienna paste, which is now generally used instead
of caustic potash. With respect to the risk of
causing peritonitis, no facts have been brought forward in support of this statement.

The possibility of not producing adhesion between the abdominal parietes and the tumour is a much more serious objection. It appears probable, however, that in those cases in which the application of the caustic failed to procure adhesion, the want of success was attributable either to the improper management of the case, or to the circumstance that the opening was effected too soon, by the additional employment of a trocar and canula.

It is evident that, in order to procure sufficient adhesion, the action of the caustic must extend to the tumour itself, and that the number of applications must be proportioned to the thickness of the structures through which the perforation is to be effected. In the successful cases detailed by Dr. Davaine the average number of applications was four or five, with an interval of one, two, or more days between the applications of the caustic.

An incision into the cicatrix, or the removal of a portion of it, before each fresh employment of the caustic, will greatly accelerate the process, whilst it will also, at the same time, enable the operator to ascertain the extent to which the parts have been destroyed.

Until recently, it was generally supposed that the opening of a cyst situated in an internal organ, and especially in the liver, would always lead to the death of the patient ; and, although experience has proved that this opinion is no longer tenable, the question has been raised whether, in the case of a hydatid tumour which does not give rise to any grave symptoms, nor to any inconvenience to the patient, it is not preferable to postpone operative interference.

It has been advanced, in favour of this delay, that the patient may still live ten, fifteen, or even twenty years, and that the natural termination of his existence may arrive before the tumour has produced any ill-results.   It is certainly true that, by the performance of an operation, some risk of shortening the patient's life is incurred ; but, on the other hand, we cannot prognosticate that the growth of the tumour will be so slow that several years may elapse before serious complications present themselves ; the long duration of life which has been stated above is only exceptional in such cases, and, if we take the average duration of life in the cases in which hydatid tumours have become apparent, it will be seen that the death of the patient may be expected within a period of from fifteen months to four years after the affection has been diagnosed, unless some means be resorted to for the removal of the hydatids.   Besides this, the older a tumour of this kind has become, the more doubtful must be the success of any plan of treatment ; and the danger of any operation is incomparably greater when the walls of the cyst have lost their elasticity and have become cartilaginous or osseous, when its cavity is filled with an atheromatous deposit, and when the neighbouring viscera have become unfitted for the performance of their functions, owing to the compression to which they have been subjected.   It should also be borne in mind that an individual who has a hydatid tumour in the chest or in the abdomen, is always liable to the danger of rupture of the tumour, as a result of some muscular effort, of external violence, or even of the progress of the affection, and to the risk of serious inflammation of an important organ, or of a large serous cavity.

The state of the tumour, its situation and its relations, and the condition of the neighbouring parts, will guide the operator in the choice of the most appropriate method of operation.

When the cyst contains a limpid fluid, and its walls are thin and elastic, a simple puncture will completely liberate the liquid if the hydatid be single, and a cure may thus be obtained. Successive punctures will be indicated when the tumour is of very considerable size. If the hydatids be multiple, a simple puncture will be insufficient; and the injection of alcohol, or of tincture of iodine, will form an useful addition to the treatment.

It may be presumed that the hydatid is single, or multiple, according to the relative quantity of fluid which is withdrawn, as compared with the size of the tumour previous to the operation.

If the tumour contains thick atheromatous matter, and the remains of a large number of hydatids, and if the walls are hard, cartilaginous, or osseous, a large aperture should be made for the escape of the cystic contents; under these circumstances, puncture with a good-sized trocar, incision, or cauterization with Vienna paste should be employed. Suction by means of a syringe, or drainage tube, and the injection of a full stream of water, or of an iodised solution, will constitute the treatment to be adopted subsequently to the operation.

The age of the tumour, and in some instances the age of the patient,—the cretaceous deposition appearing to be more frequent in old than in young persons,—will assist the practitioner in judging whether the hydatid cyst has undergone modifications of structure, and whether its contents have become atheromatous ; in doubtful cases, an exploratory puncture will render the diagnosis more satisfactory.

The hydatid cysts of the face, of the neck, and of superficial parts of the body should be opened by incision.

It is important to open promptly the cysts which are situated in the anterior part of the neck, in consequence of their tendency to perforate the trachea or other important passages, or to form a connection with the thyroid gland.

Incision is also indicated when a hydatid tumour, which was primarily developed in an internal organ, extends to the surface of the body, especially if its projection, and a digital examination, together with the redness of the surrounding integuments, further lead to the opinion that the cyst has contracted adhesions with the walls of the large cavity within which it is contained.

Operations upon hydatid cysts situated within the chest have been too few in number to enable us to decide what would be the best method of treatment. Those cases which have been recorded tend to show that the pleural layers are usually united by adhesions, so that effusion of the cystic contents into the serous cavity need seldom be feared. Dr. Davaine gives the details of five cases of intra-thoracic hydatid cysts ; two of these were opened by the bistoury, two by puncture, and one was treated by puncture with the subsequent injection of a solution

of iodine ; each of these methods furnished one case
of cure.

Most of what has been already said respecting
the different methods of treatment has reference
to the hydatid cysts developed in the abdominal
cavity, and especially in the liver ; in such cases the
danger of effusion into the peritoneum constitutes
the chief difficulty of any operation performed for
their removal. Puncture, or simple incision, may be
performed when the cysts are united to the abdominal
walls by adhesions ; but if there be no adhesions, it
will be necessary to leave the canula in the opening
after having recourse to puncture, or to gradually
destroy the coverings of the tumour, and to produce
the formation of adhesions by the application of
caustics.

When the ordinary signs of adhesion, such as
tumefaction, redness, &c., are absent, it is difficult to
form a correct opinion as to whether any adhesions
exist between the cyst and the abdominal parietes.
Two methods of determining this question have been
suggested.

In the first, the patient having been placed upon
his left side, a line is to be traced with ink along the
lower border of the liver or of the tumour ; then, by
causing him to repeatedly change his position, and
to make deep efforts of respiration, we may observe,
if there be no adhesion, variations in the relative
situation of the line traced upon the integument and
the position of the edge of the liver, or of the
tumour.

According to the second plan, the patient is to
be placed upon the side opposite to that on which

the tumour is situated, and we may judge that adhesions exist between the cyst and the abdominal parietes if the tumour does not become further distant from the point where it was most projecting, and where it appeared to adhere, and if the fluctuation also continues to be felt at the same point.

In the case of hydatids developed in the bones, the operation of opening the pouch which encloses the vesicular worms is not usually sufficient ; and the disorganization of the bony tissue, the implication of the neighbouring structures, and the impossibility of procuring union of the walls of the cyst, sometimes render either resection or amputation necessary. When the hydatids are situated in a flat bone, the total extirpation of the tumour is occasionally requisite, as the hydatids of bones are not always collected into a single cyst, but, on the contrary, often occupy separate cells disseminated throughout the structure of the bone.

After hydatid cysts have been opened, it is important to prevent the entrance of air into the cavity, and also the putrefaction of that portion of the contents which has not been evacuated, so as to obviate the consequences which might result from the absorption of putrid matter.

Two conditions are necessary for this purpose, namely to afford a ready means of exit for the contents of the cyst, and to substitute an antiseptic fluid for the putrescent matter.

If the cyst only contains clear liquid, the primary aperture, even if it were only made with a capillary trocar, might be sufficient to accomplish the first-named indication ; but if the walls of the cyst be hard and cretaceous, or if its contents have become atheromatous, the opening must be made of a larger size. The discharge of the matter through the opening might also be assisted by the injection of a full stream of water into the cyst, or by suction with a syringe.

The second indication may be fulfilled by the injection of various liquids, which possess an anti-putrescent property. The decoction of barley, of marsh-mallow, and of cinchona, warm water, wine, alcohol diluted with water, chlorinated water, solution of iodine, and bile, have been employed in different cases.

The injection of fluids supposed to be capable of destroying the vesicular worms, and of promoting the gradual contraction and cure of the cyst, by modifying the nature of its internal surface, has also been resorted to. The liquids which have been chiefly employed with this view are alcohol, bile, and solutions containing iodine.

The iodised injections have been used, after either a simple puncture, or puncture and incision through a cicatrix, or simple incision into the tumour. The quantity of the injection would vary according to the size of the cyst; and it should be composed of tincture of iodine and distilled water, in equal proportions, to which might be advantageously added a small quantity of iodide of potassium.[1] The injection should be allowed to remain in the cyst, which has,

---

[1] In two successful cases, operated upon by M. Aran, the injection consisted of about one ounce and a half of tincture of iodine, the same amount of distilled water, and thirty grains of iodide of potassium.

of course, been previously emptied as nearly as possible of its contents ; if symptoms of iodism make their appearance, they soon disappear again, and in favourable cases no bad complications whatever need be feared.

Dr. Davaine gives an analysis of fourteen cases treated by the use of iodised injections. In eight of these it formed the principal part of the treatment ; in four of the eight cases, the cure was due to the employment of the injection ; on three occasions the injection was unattended with success, and incision was subsequently performed ; in one case death followed the operation, but it was attributable to other causes than the plan of treatment which was adopted. In the other six cases the injections were only employed as accessory to other methods of treatment,— twice after repeated puncture, once after incision into the tumour, and three times after the application of caustic ; good results occurred in three of these cases ; in one death supervened, and the subsequent history of the other two cases is insufficient to show what the final results of the operation were.

Alcoholic injections have been employed in two cases of hydatids with perfect success. In one of these, a case of hydatids of the liver, caustic potash was first applied, and the cicatrix was afterwards incised, so as to liberate a considerable number of hydatids ; the operator, M. Jobert, then injected a mixture of alcohol and distilled water into the cyst, and allowed a female catheter to remain in the wound in order to facilitate the escape of the fluid and of the hydatids ; hydatids continued to be discharged through the opening for two months after the operation, and the patient was eventually cured. In a similar case, under the charge of M. Richard, the tumour was opened by means of a puncture, and two drachms of pure alcohol were injected into the cyst, after its contents had been discharged, and before the canula was withdrawn; acute pain was produced, but it subsided after a few minutes; the case progressed favourably, and in three months afterwards no traces of the tumour remained.

The injection of bile into the interior of hydatid cysts has been recently proposed, upon two different grounds; one, that the contact with the biliary fluid would kill the hydatids; and the other, founded upon a case of hepatic cyst, in which the bile flowed abundantly into the abscess and the pus soon ceased to be formed, that the bile possesses an antiseptic property. The only instance of the actual injection of bile occurred in the practice of M. Voisin; the repeated injections of the ox-gall, which was used, did not give rise to any pain, and no symptoms of purulent infection presented themselves, but the patient unfortunately died of pneumonia about a month afterwards. At the post-mortem examination of the body, the internal surface of the cyst was found to be smooth, and of a very healthy appearance; it had considerably diminished in size.

CHAPTER XXVI.

THE CYSTICERCUS TELÆ CELLULOSÆ.

THE Cysticercus telæ cellulosæ[1] is the only species of the cysticerci which need be described here.

Like the hydatids, it is commonly enclosed in a cyst formed of areolar tissue, which is more or less condensed, according to the nature of the organ in which it is developed; it is usually solitary. The cyst may undergo modification of structure, and may acquire greater consistence and thickness, in proportion to the length of time during which it has existed; the vesicular worm itself experiences various changes, the termination of which is that it is probably destroyed, whilst its empty and modified cyst remains. Laennec, having observed vesicles in the liver of a person in whom cysticerci were found in several organs of the body, considered that these vesicles were the cysts of former cysticerci; analogous facts which have been remarked in the instance of hydatids, and certain nematoid worms of which the cysts remain after the entozoa have been destroyed, and the striking alterations which have been demonstrated in cysticerci of old standing, conduce to render this view very probably a correct one.

This species of cysticercus is most frequently met with in the intermuscular areolar tissue of the trunk, of the limbs, of the heart, and of the intestines, in

---

[1] The name of this species of Cysticercus is derived from the circumstance of its being found in the areolar, or as it was formerly termed cellular, tissue. The word "telæ," although grammatically necessary, is commonly omitted by writers.

the brain and its membranes, in the lung, and in the eye; it is also sometimes found in a serous cavity, when its cyst may be absent.

The cysticerci occasionally exist in very large numbers, and they then give rise to serious morbid phenomena. In other instances, they may not produce any special pathological symptoms, unless they are developed in the nervous centres, in the eye, or in the larynx; and if we except those cases in which their presence may be ascertained by direct inspection (as when they are situated beneath the tongue, or in the eye) there are no fully reliable signs of their existence.

The circumstances which determine, and even those which are favourable to, the development of the cysticerci are still unknown; it it probable, however, that they depend, to a certain extent, upon the manner of living of the affected individual.

The animals in which the presence of the cysticercus telæ cellulosæ has been ascertained, besides Man, are the pig, the dog, the monkey, the bear, the goat, and the rat. The pig is more subject than any other animal to the attacks of this entozoon, which produces the unhealthy state of the flesh usually spoken of as "measled," or "measly" pork in this country; this disease is known under the name of "Ladrerie" in France, where it is exceedingly common. This affection of the porcine tribe is very widely spread, and has been observed not only in Europe, but also in America.[1]

[1] In a paper read before the Royal Dublin Society, at the December meeting, 1862, upon the Prevalence and Prevention of Diseases amongst Domestic Animals, Professor Gamgee, of the

According to the cases which have been collected, the parts of the human body in which cysticerci have been most frequently observed are :—1. The inter-muscular areolar tissue of the body and of the extremities ; 2. The brain ; and 3. The eye. The spleen and the kidneys appear to be exempt from the cysticercus telæ cellulosæ, and the liver is also very rarely invaded by this entozoon.

Similarly to the hydatids, cysticerci have a ten-dency to dissemination throughout the body, and they may often be seen in several organs, both superficial and deep, in the same individual. It is a remarkable fact that these two genera of vesicular worms have, to some extent, an inverse tendency in their distribution ; hydatids are common in the liver, in the lungs, and in the abdominal viscera ; the cysticerci are, on the contrary, rare in these organs, but are frequent in the parietes of the body, in the limbs, in the brain, and in the eye, which parts are very seldom invaded by hydatids.

The cysticercus found in Man has been observed in different countries and climates. It does not appear to be more often present in one sex than in the other ; and it has been seen in children not less frequently than in adults. According to Rudolphi, vesicular worms are more common in persons of a leucophlegmatic diathesis than in others.

Veterinary College, Edinburgh, stated that 3 per cent. of the pigs in Ireland are "measly," owing to improper management. As the cysticercus telæ cellulosæ is now generally supposed to be converted into tape-worm, after it has found its way into the human intestines, the serious ill effects which result from the use of the flesh of these diseased animals as an article of food can scarcely be sufficiently estimated.

CHAPTER XXVII.

ENTOZOA DEVELOPED IN THE CENTRAL NERVOUS SYSTEM.

THE invasion of the central nervous system by entozoa is not rare in Man and in herbivorous mammiferæ. These entozoa belong exclusively to the three genera of vesicular worms, of which only two, the hydatid and the cysticercus, can be considered to exist in the human subject, no well-authenticated instance having been recorded of the occurrence of the cœnurus in Man.[1]

The pathological phenomena produced by hydatids and by cysticerci present important distinctions. The indefinite increase in size of the former, and the very considerable bulk to which they attain, must sooner or later give rise to serious, and even mortal, complications. The cysticerci, which never become very large, may continue for a long time almost innocuous.

These entozoa are situated, sometimes externally, sometimes internally, as regards the encephalon, and they may also be developed at any portion of the

---

[1] Although the cœnurus, like the hydatids or the cysticerci, may be contained within a serous cavity, the cyst which encloses it never exists excepting in some part of the encephalon, and the cœnurus must consequently be regarded as an entozoon peculiar to the nervous system. It is the only entozoon which is known to have its *habitat* exclusively in the nervous centres. It is more frequent in the sheep than in any other animal, and it produces in the sheep a very peculiar epileptiform affection, to which the name of " Staggers " is commonly applied in agricultural districts.

whole extent of the cerebro-spinal axis.   The
hydatids will be first described, and the cysticerci
subsequently.

The cyst, or pouch, of hydatids developed in the
brain is single in the majority of cases.   Its bulk,
which is very variable, may equal that of a hen's egg,
or it may even exceed that size ; in a case, observed
by Headington, recorded in the "Edinburgh Medical
and 'Surgical Journal" (vol. xv, page 504), the pouch
contained a pound of fluid, and in another case,
which came under the notice of Rendtorf, a mass of
hydatids, weighing two and a half pounds, was found
within the pouch.   The hydatid pouch in the brain
encloses, similarly to cysts in other organs, sometimes
only one large hydatid, and sometimes a great number
of these bodies, of variable dimensions.

When the pouches which enclose the hydatids are
multiple, the patient necessarily perishes before they
have acquired any considerable size.   In illustration
of this fact, a very interesting case, described by
Calmeil, Physician to the Lunatic Asylum at Charen-
ton, may be quoted ; it is that of an officer in the
army, who, until within a short time before his
admission, was in possession of perfect health ; in
the course of a few months, the patient died, his
intellectual faculties, and sensory and motor functions having been successively lost; when a post-
mortem examination was made, almost innumerable
small acephalocysts were found scattered upon the
surface, and in the interior, of the brain.

The hydatid pouch in the brain is formed, as far
as may be judged from the observations which have
been made, by a depression of the cerebral substance,

lined by a delicate layer of areolar tissue, which may be regarded as a true cyst; in some few cases, however, the hydatids were probably developed in a free condition, either in the cavity of the arachnoid, or in that of the ventricles. The hydatids which are developed in the brain-substance itself, appear to be deficient of an envelope of areolar tissue, and to be in immediate relation with the cerebral substance. Those which have their primitive seat in the pia-mater, or in the choroid plexuses, are always contained within a more or less complete cyst. The cyst is very delicate, possesses only a slight degree of firmness, and is thicker at its free portion than where it is in contact with the cerebral tissue.

The hydatids, as their development continues, compress the neighbouring parts of the brain, which becomes atrophied, and is sometimes reduced, in the vicinity of the hydatid tumour, to the state of a thin membrane. The nerves, which are in relation with the cyst, in any part of their course, are similarly atrophied; and, in some instances, the bony parietes of the cranium have been known to suffer from the effects of the enlargement of the hydatid tumour, and to undergo local dilatation, together with atrophy and absorption, in consequence of the continuous and increasing pressure of the tumour.

Under these latter circumstances, the hydatids may possibly find a means of exit, and the cure of a disease, which might be generally expected to prove mortal, might thus be obtained. An instance of this, referred to by Dr. Davaine, occurred in the hospital at Bordeaux. In such cases, it would be advisable to accelerate the discharge of the hydatid fluid and of the vesicular worms by the performance of the operation of trephining.

The progressive and gradual compression exerted by the hydatid tumours does not at first produce any other effects than those which have been already mentioned; but, after a time, new lesions present themselves. These may be of a local character, and occur chiefly around the tumour, such as congestion, inflammation, softening, or induration; or they may be more general, such as sub-arachnoidean effusion, serous infiltration into the cavities of the ventricles or into the cavity of the arachnoid membrane, and cerebral hæmorrhage.

Upon a consideration of the symptoms, and of the appearances found on making post-mortem examinations, it is evident that the hydatid tumour must sometimes have reached a very large bulk before the production of any marked functional derangement. In this respect, as in that of the anatomical lesions which they occasion, the hydatids of the nervous centres do not differ from any other species of intra-cranial tumour, which has a slow development, and ultimately attains to a large size.

The principal and most frequent symptoms of hydatid tumours situated in the brain are headache, convulsive paroxysms, vomiting, syncope, and disturbance of the motor and sensory functions, and of the intellectual faculties.

Headache is a very common, and often the first, symptom; it is sometimes continuous, but more generally it occurs in paroxysms; it is very severe occasionally, and usually becomes more marked as the affection advances. Neuralgic pains, simulating rheumatism, are also experienced in other parts of the body, especially in the muscles.

Vomiting is frequently one of the earliest symptoms of cerebral hydatid tumours, and is also one of the most persistent, and of the least amenable to treatment.

Repeated fits of syncope, giddiness, and convulsive paroxysms often occur at the commencement of the affection, and continue throughout its whole course. The convulsions, which return at variable intervals, sometimes assume an epileptic character.

The injury to the motor functions is manifested by the appearance of hemiplegia, or of paraplegia; these complications have been known to come on suddenly with great severity, but they are more usually ushered in by feebleness of the limbs, which becomes gradually more marked, until the patient is partially or completely paralysed. Simultaneously with the destruction of the motor power, a progressively advancing diminution of one or more of the senses will be observable.

Paralysis is one of the most common phenomena, but when the hydatids are of small size, and are disseminated throughout various parts of the encephalon, it does not come on until an advanced stage of the affection. The paralytic symptoms, taken as a whole, usually differ from those which characterise an acute disorder of one of the hemispheres of the brain; in fact, owing to its situation, and its great bulk, the hydatid tumour compresses both of the lateral halves of the brain, and frequently also some of the cranial nerves; a group of peculiar symptoms, some of which are rarely to be found associated with the ordinary affections of the brain, are the results of this extensive lesion. The accidental complications which supervene after some time, such as sanguineous or serous effusion, softening of the brain, &c., also vary the symptomatic character of the disease.

Disturbance of the intellect, loss of the mental faculties, and mania or dementia, may mark the presence of hydatids; either from the commencement of the affection, or only towards the period of its termination ; in some cases, however, which have been recorded, the intellect remained perfectly sound.

The progress of an hydatid tumour, when no new lesion of the brain occurs, is always slow ; and its duration, which cannot be definitely determined, may be for several months, or even for several years. The situation of the tumour must necessarily produce very great differences in the length of time during which the affection lasts, just as it does in the appearance, and in the nature, of the symptoms.

Generally speaking, the symptoms become gradually worse, and the patient dies comatose ; in other cases, cerebral softening, apoplexy, or serous effusion, terminate the malady. Recovery is a rare termination, excepting when an opportunity can be afforded for the removal of the hydatids by trephining.

The invariably small size of the cysticerci, and their frequent multiplicity, produce important differences in the symptoms to which they give rise, and in the succession and progress of these symptoms, as compared with the corresponding pathological effects which result from the presence of hydatids.

The cysticerci developed in the brain sometimes exist in great numbers, either accumulated in one part only or, as is more generally the case, disseminated throughout the whole encephalon. In the majority of cases, the cysticerci are situated in the cerebral substance, in the pia-mater, and in the choroid plexuses; they are also occasionally found in the membranes of the brain.

Like the hydatids, the cysticerci are invested by a delicate covering of areolar tissue, which serves the purpose of a cyst for them; when they are situated in the interior of the brain, the cyst is very fine, or consists only of a few filamentous shreds.

The cysticerci situated in the brain are often found to have undergone marked changes of structure. The vesicle becomes more globular, and is occasionally divided into lobules, or into two distinct portions; the head, the rostellum, and the suckers of the entozoon are covered by a deposit of black, pigmentary matter; at a more advanced period the hooks diminish in number, or even disappear altogether; the contracted or obliterated opening of the vesicle does not permit of the protrusion of the body, and the head, which is invaginated in the latter, can only be extracted from it by careful pressure.

These changes bear an evident relation to the age of the cysticerci. The differences which they produce in the appearance of these entozoa have been regarded as natural to their growth by some helminthologists, whilst other writers have considered them as sufficiently characteristic to admit of the classification of the cysticerci into several species. (*Vide* "Synopsis," page 19.)

The fact that such alterations have been observed
in cysticerci found in persons who presented symptoms of cerebral disorder only a few days previously
to their decease, is a proof that cysticerci, may exist
for a considerable period without giving rise to
marked complications ; and it may be readily understood that, when they are situated in the pia-mater,
or in the choroid plexuses, and limited to a small
bulk, they can have only a slight action upon the
brain-substance itself, whilst it may also be seen
that, unless they are accumulated in great numbers
at one spot, they will not exert sufficient compression
upon the brain for the abolition of its functions.   In
this respect, observation agrees with theory, as may
be ascertained upon an examination into the recorded
cases of cysticerci in the brain.

The pathological phenomena produced by the
presence of cysticerci in the brain may be either
chronic or acute.   In the chronic state, epileptiform
attacks have been known to come on at distant
intervals, together with monomaniacal delirium, hebe-
tude of the faculties, or dementia.   After a duration
of several years, without any marked change being
perceived in the condition of the patient, the preceding symptoms are suddenly replaced, or masked,
by the appearance of new symptoms which are caused,
either by the irritation produced by the tumour, or by
inflammation of the brain or its membranes, or by
sanguineous, or serous effusion.   These new symptoms are general or partial convulsions, delirium,
strong mental disturbance, fever, and coma, &c.,
which usually destroy the patient in the course of a
few days.

In other cases, the existence of cysticerci in the brain was not manifested by any particular sign, until the symptoms of an acute affection of that organ made their appearance. In these instances, severe headache, convulsions of the extremities and of the lower jaw, great rapidity of the pulse, difficulty of breathing, exhaustion, and coma followed one another in quick succession, and the death of the patient occurred at the end of a few weeks, or even days.

Vesicular worms which are developed in the spinal canal, or which find their way into it from without, give rise sooner or later to the phenomena which result from gradual and increasing compression of the spinal cord, arising from any cause whatever ; so that they do not consequently differ from the symptoms which are observed when any foreign body exists in the spinal cord or canal.

There will be loss of motion and of sensation in the parts which are situated below the seat of the tumour, constipation, and retention or incontinence of urine ; and these symptoms are commonly pre-ceded by pain, convulsive attacks, and a sense of tingling and irritation in the extremities.

The pain may be very acute, and be confined to the part occupied by the tumour, or it may follow the course of the large nervous trunks, and come on in paroxysms, accompanied by cramps or spasmodic convulsions in the limbs, which soon lose both sensa-tion and the power of voluntary motion.

The paralysis generally attacks the lower extre-mities, the bladder, and the rectum, but it may, of course, extend to other parts if the tumour be situated near the upper portion of the spinal cord ;

for instance, one of the arms may be affected, or there may be great difficulty of breathing, which becomes gradually worse.

The disease which is produced by vesicular worms in the spinal cord or canal has been known to last over several months, and even several years, until the patient's constitution is finally undermined, sores form upon the sacrum, and other parts of the body, and the patient dies of exhaustion.

Chapter XXVIII.

ENTOZOA IN THE MUSCULAR SYSTEM.

The Trichina Spiralis.

The Trichina spiralis, which exists in the human body, may be regarded as special to the muscular system of animal life, for it has never been found in any other muscles than those which possess striated fibres.

This entozoon appears, probably on account of its very small size, to have escaped notice until about thirty or forty years since, when it attracted the attention of several English and German anatomists. Its name was given to it by Professor Owen, who made a careful examination into the nature of this parasite in 1835. Since this period, Professor Owen states that he has met with several cases in which the T. spiralis was present ; and, so far is it from being uncommon, that during the last five years, evidence of the attacks of this entozoon have been remarked in 2 per cent. of the subjects dissected in the Anatomy Rooms of the University of Edinburgh.

The trichina is a nematoid worm, about $\frac{1}{30}$th of an inch in length, and $\frac{1}{700}$th of an inch in diameter. It is always enclosed in a cyst, of which the long axis lies between, and parallel to the direction of, the fibres of the muscle ; about one-third of this cyst is occupied by the entozoon, which is rolled up spirally, forming two or three spiral turns, whence the name given to it by Professor Owen is partly derived. It is usually solitary, although in some rare instances two, and sometimes even three, trichinæ have been found within one cyst.

Fig. 14.[1]

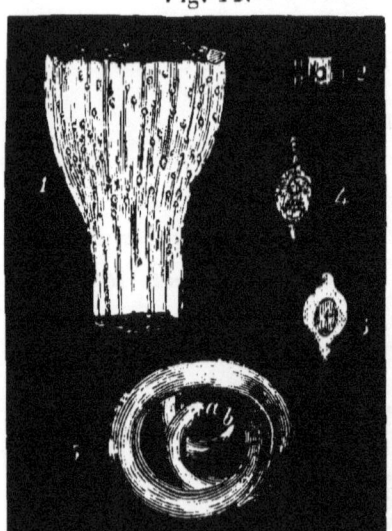

The cyst is generally an ovoid vesicle presenting a prolongation at one, or both, of its extremities, so that it has a spindle-shaped appearance. The dimensions of the cyst are very variable, as is also the thickness of its walls. According to Owen, and most other observers, it

[1] Fig. 14.—1. A portion of the biceps muscle of the arm, studded with the cysts of the Trichina spiralis. 2. A single cyst. 3. A cyst magnified twenty times, and containing calcareous matter. 4. A cyst containing two worms. 5. A trichina magnified two hundred times ; a, the head ; b, the tail.

is composed of two distinct vesicles, an external one, which gives it its fusiform appearance, and which constitutes the prolongations at either end, and an internal one, which is usually oval, and is not elongated at the extremities like the outer vesicle.

Numerous opinions have been advanced respecting the nature of these vesicles. Professor Owen says that they are homogeneous, and are constituted by layers of condensed areolar tissue, which he considers to be produced from the human tissues; other observers state that the two vesicles have a different structure; whilst others, again, including Dr. Bristowe and Mr. Rainey, believe that the cyst is single, and is exclusively the product of the trichina.

The walls of the cyst abound in numerous elementary granules of an earthy character. Its cavity contains a substance which is frequently opaque, and consists of refractive globules, of different sizes, suspended in a viscid fluid; no cells, nor nuclei have ever been observed in this substance, in which the entozoon is, as it were, embedded.

Trichinæ are not found in all of the cysts, and those which do exist are in a condition of development, or of alteration, or are completely modified in their characteristics and destroyed. The death of a trichina is followed by the deposition of earthy matter, chiefly composed of carbonate of lime, in the body of the worm and the surrounding space.

Trichinæ have been observed in nearly all of the muscles which possess striated fibres, with the exception of the heart. The number of these parasites is most extraordinary in some cases; and they have been known to be so universally disseminated throughout the body that even the smallest muscles, such as those of the larynx and of the eye, were invaded by them. They are generally more numerous in the superficial than in the deep-seated muscles, and have been more frequently met with in the pectoralis major and the latissimus dorsi muscles than elsewhere.

The parts which are affected by the trichina are studded with small white spots which may be easily recognised as vesicles, when they are placed beneath the microscope ; and the worms may then be seen coiled up in the interior of the vesicles. The cysts are arranged, sometimes in groups, and sometimes in a linear series, in the muscular tissue ; occasionally they are isolated.

The long diameter of the cysts is always parallel to the course of the muscular fibres ; and they adhere loosely to the surrounding areolar tissue, excepting at their prolonged extremities which are always more firmly attached. The muscular fibres, situated in the immediate vicinity of the cysts, are often covered with an oily-albuminous matter ; in other respects, however, they may present a healthy appearance.

The trichina spiralis has been observed in Europe, and in America. The largest number of cases have been met with in Great Britain, but this greater proportional frequency may be probably due to the fact that attention was first directed in this country to this peculiar entozoon.

According to the cases which have been hitherto published, it is evident that the presence of the trichina bears no relation to the age or sex of the

individuals affected by it.   Nothing definite is yet
known respecting the causes and the conditions upon
which the attacks of this parasite depend.[1]

Contrary to what might be expected, the persons
in whom trichinæ have been found after death did
not in the majority of cases complain of pain, or of
any particular symptom which could be assigned to
the presence of these worms ; their existence might
consequently be unattended by serious results, at
any rate for some time, as they are not reproduced
in the muscular structure (owing to their not being
provided with organs of reproduction), and as they
always perish before they acquire very considerable
dimensions.   They leave behind them the cysts, in
and around which cretaceous matter and particles of
fat are deposited.

In some few instances, sub-acute pain and feverish-
ness have marked the invasion of trichinæ, but not
to such an extent as to be decisively diagnostic of

---

[1] It has been suggested by Leuckart, and some other German
writers, that the young trichinæ having found their way accidentally, like other entozoa, into the alimentary canal, subsequently
pierce the intestinal walls, and, guided by the intermuscular con-
nective tissue, reach the interior of the muscular fasciculus, where
their development is continued.   This opinion is highly hypo-
thetical, especially as no lesion of the intestinal walls has been
found upon making a post-mortem examination ; besides which it
would be difficult to reconcile these views with the observations
which have been made respecting the action of other entozoa
upon the walls of the intestines, and with the fact that the
trichinæ are almost always more abundant in the superficial than
in the deep-seated muscles.

The supposition that the existence of the trichinæ is probably
connected with the employment of diseased flesh, such as measly
pork, as an article of food, is partly in accordance with theory
and the results of experimentation.

the affection. If the cause of the malady be suspected during the lifetime of the individual, a microscopic examination should be made of a portion of the muscular tissue.

Until our knowledge of the manner in which the trichina is introduced into the body is more extended, the plan of treatment which ought to be adopted must be necessarily uncertain. Küchenmeister advises the use of purgatives, and of frequent small doses of oil of turpentine with powdered fernroot. From the circumstance that the superficial muscles are those which are most often affected, I should be disposed to resort, in addition to the method recommended by Küchenmeister, to the employment of fumigations or baths containing sulphur, or some similar remedial agent which might possibly be absorbed into the body in a sufficient quantity to cause the destruction of the entozoa.

Chapter XXIX.

ENTOZOA FOUND IN THE SUBCUTANEOUS AND INTERORGANIC AREOLAR TISSUE.

The Filaria Medinensis.

Synonyms:—Dracunculus; Guinea-worm.

This is a nematoid parasite, which is only observed in the inhabitants of intertropical regions, and especially in the natives of some parts of Asia and

of Africa, where it is endemic, and occasionally
epidemic.   Its frequent occurrence upon the coast of
Guinea has originated the common English name.

It is a very slender, round worm, of almost uniform dimensions throughout its whole extent; and
varies from a few inches to four or five feet in length.
It attacks the superficial portions of the lower
extremities, and it is also sometimes to be met with
in the subcutaneous areolar tissue of the body, of the
upper extremities, and, in very rare instances, of
different parts of the head and face.   It is not contained within a cyst, but lives in a free state in the
tissues, and finds its way readily beneath the skin,
and between the vessels, nerves, and muscles, or
even into the substance of the latter.   It is often
solitary, but several filariæ may exist simultaneously
or successively in the same individual.

The conditions upon which the appearance and
the propagation of the Guinea-worm appear most to
depend are moisture and the excessive heat of the
countries in which this entozoon prevails; and the
united influence of these causes serves to explain the
greater relative frequency of the F. Medinensis at
some seasons of the year than at others.

The filaria which is developed in the human body
shows signs of life for a short period only after its
extraction, and soon perishes; so that it evidently does
not possess in itself the means of transmission and
of propagation.   At the time when this entozoon has
completed its development, and is ready to leave the
organism in which its development has taken place,
its body is found to be filled with a milky-looking
substance, which, upon microscopic examination, may

be ascertained to be chiefly constituted by the agglomeration of an immense number of very minute embryos, which are invisible to the naked eye, when they are inspected singly. These embryos can live for an indefinite period in water at the ordinary temperature of European countries, and they are capable of exhibiting lively movements after they have been kept dry for many hours, if they are again moistened with water.[1]

It is, therefore, probable that, at the heat which is always maintained in intertropical countries, these embryos may live for a long period in water at a high temperature, and may also remain in a state of desiccation for a considerable space of time without the loss of their vitality. These points have not been fully investigated ; but, whatever may be the extent of the property which the embryo possesses of living for a certain period out of the human body, it is certainly to it that the Guinea-worm owes its means of transmission ; in fact the larvæ, either living in the water of the lakes or rivers, into which they have been carried through the medium of the dust, or revivified by the agency of the rain when they are situated upon the soil, may after a long interval be placed in a position suitable to their introduction into the tissues where they subsequently become developed.

The question has been raised, whether the embryos which are expelled from the body of the parent-filaria can at once introduce themselves into

[1] Similar phenomena have been observed in the embryos of certain small nematoid worms which live in insects like the filariæ do in man.

the tissues, and continue their development in that situation. Dr. Davaine observes that this may be answered negatively for two reasons; the first, that the rupture of a filaria whilst situated within the human body is not followed by a new generation of filariæ; and the second, that the Guinea-worm is not propagated in countries which are situated much to the north of the tropics, although the larvæ may be kept alive for several days by placing them in water. According to these facts, it may be considered probable that the embryo must acquire a certain degree of development externally to the human body before its introduction into it, so as to attain the adult state, and also that the tropical heat is requisite for the accomplishment of that part of its development which takes place before it finds its way into the body.

It is generally acknowledged by the writers who have had ample opportunities for the observation of the attacks of the Guinea-worm, that its appearance and relative frequency are in some manner connected with the heavy periodical rains, with the degree of humidity of the locality, and with the extent and position of the marshes and rivers; but these authors do not agree as to the mode in which the filaria enters the human tissues.

Some have strongly upheld the opinion that the larvæ of the filaria are taken into the stomach with the water which is employed for drinking purposes, and that they then penetrate amongst the tissues so as to reach the situation in which they are ultimately found; but this opinion is scarcely tenable, however, when it is considered that the ordinary seat of the

Guinea-worm is in the superficial parts of the body, and especially of the lower extremities, and it is highly probable that the entozoon finds its way through the integuments.

Cases have been recorded by some authors of persons who, although they have not drunk the water of the countries infested by the Guinea-worm, have yet been affected by it; other observers have stated that, amongst a large body of men the officers who did not walk, nor lay upon the ground, with the legs bare, were not affected with the parasite, whilst nearly all of the common soldiers who were less careful in their habits, and walked about without shoes to their feet, were attacked by the Guinea-worm, after a time;[1] and Dr. Chisholm has reported a fact which, of itself, is a sufficient support for the belief that the larval worms are introduced through the skin, namely, that the *Bheesties* (native water-carriers in India) who carry the water in leathern vessels resting upon their backs and shoulders, are most frequently affected by the Guinea-worm in those parts of the body which are brought into contact with the vessels, and the water which is spilt from them.

A consideration of the relative size of the pores of the skin, and of the very minute embryos of the filaria, shows that it is possible that the young filariæ may obtain an entrance through the pores into the subcutaneous areolar tissue.

[1] See a short paper by Mr. Heath, "Observations on the Generation of the Guinea-worm," in the "Edinburgh Medical Journal," vol. xii, p. 120. That writer also mentions the important fact that both officers and men drank of the same water, although none of the former were affected.

In the countries where the Guinea-worm is common, all of the inhabitants, without distinction as to age or sex, or to the race or country to which they may have originally belonged, are alike subject to its attacks. Sometimes its appearance constitutes an actual epidemic; in a letter to Clot-Bey, Dr. Marrudri states that in the Egyptian expedition into Cordofan in 1820, one-fourth of the whole army was suddenly affected by this entozoon, and that he himself suffered from its attacks in no less than twenty-eight different parts of his body successively; and in some districts one-half of the entire population have been known to be affected by Guinea-worm. Europeans sometimes suffer severely from this scourge; Sir James M'Gregor records that three hundred soldiers out of one regiment, the 86th, stationed at Bombay, were attacked by Guinea-worm during the monsoon season; this regiment was replaced by the 88th, and one hundred and sixty men out of three hundred and sixty were subsequently affected by the same entozoon.

The number of filariæ which exist in one person is very variable, and may range from one or two up to as many as thirty or forty.

This parasite usually invades the lower extremities, and is seldom found in the upper extremities, the trunk of the body, or the face; it is not met with in the viscera of the chest or of the abdomen. An analysis made by Sir James M'Gregor of 181 cases, shows that the feet and legs were affected in 157 of the whole number.

Generally speaking, the Guinea-worm is superficially situated, and occupies the subcutaneous areolar tissue, when it is distinguishable both to the sight and the touch, and resembles a small cord, extending spirally beneath the integument of the affected part; in some few instances it is occasionally deeply · situated amongst the muscles. When the parasite is very long, both ends of it are evident beneath the skin at some distance from each other, whilst the central portion of the worm dips down into the deep-seated structures.

It exists in the human body for a considerable period, probably of not less than two months, without giving any indication of its presence; for it does not, contrary to what might be expected, give rise to any marked symptoms until its embryos are formed. The earliest sign by which the presence of a filaria is manifested is usually an unpleasant feeling of irritation in the part of the limb which is occupied by the worm ; and a tumour, which assumes the appearance of a boil, is shortly afterwards formed in the same situation. In some cases, the formation of the tumour is preceded by general indisposition, by pains in the head or stomach, and by nausea and vomiting. When the Guinea-worm is situated in parts which are almost destitute of soft tissues, as in the toes, or near the joints, for example, it produces acute pain ; but when it is deeply seated amongst the muscles, it gives rise to a painless swelling, which may last for several weeks, or even months. In all instances, when the tumour is about to burst, the pain becomes intense, the constitution sympathises with the local disorder, the part is much inflamed, and the tumour is eventually converted into an abscess, which furnishes a means of exit for a portion of the entozoon.

The tumour is occasionally of considerable size, and the worm which is contained within it is then discharged whole; the fluid which escapes from the opening is usually of a serous character.

The diagnosis of the existence of a Guinea-worm is sometimes very difficult, and it is not until after the appearance of a portion of the filaria externally that the nature of the affection can be fully determined, as it is liable to be mistaken for an inflamed vein, or lymphatic vessel, or for some other species of tumour.

The best method of treatment consists in the gradual removal of the worm, which is effected by daily winding the protruding portion of it round a small piece of wood, or a roll of adhesive plaster, great care being taken so as not to break the worm by too forcible traction; a bandage should be employed so as to prevent the portion of the worm which is extracted from being again drawn beneath the skin. If the parasite be broken, serious results often follow, and there is great local inflammation and sympathetic fever, together with the formation of abscesses and sinuses; gangrene is sometimes produced as a consequence of the accidental rupture of the worm. These complications are attributed by some observers to the presence of dead animal matter, and by others to the escape of the embryonic filariæ into the various structures by which the adult filaria is surrounded.

Numerous medicaments have been suggested and tried both for the prevention and for the cure of the affection. Assafœtida has been especially recommended as a prophylactic, and several writers state that the use of this substance prevents the attacks of the Guinea-worm, and causes its more speedy expulsion, should it happen to be present; Bremser mentions, on the authority of Dubois, that the Brahmins, who season their food very strongly with assafœtida, are never affected by Guinea-worm. Aloes, garlic, pepper, camphor, tobacco, sulphur, and the different mercurial preparations, have all been administered internally, or applied externally; and various plants, known only to the natives of Africa and of India, are said to be successfully employed by them to produce the death of the worm.

The protection of the feet and other parts of the body against dust and moisture by means of suitable covering, ought to be always adopted in those countries in which the Guinea-worm is endemic.

CHAPTER XXX.

ENTOZOA SITUATED IN THE EYE AND ITS APPENDAGES.

THE entozoa which are found in the interior of the eye in Man, and in animals,[1] belong to those species

---

[1] Entozoa have been found in the eyes of horses, horned cattle, pigs, sheep, birds, and fishes, and most probably exist occasionally in the same situation in all other species of Vertebrata. A nematoid worm, the *filaria papillosa*, has been often met with in the anterior chamber of the eye of horses which have been permitted to graze in certain low-lying districts of India, soon after the periodical rainy season.

which live in serous cavities or in the areolar tissue of other parts of the body. Those which have been hitherto observed in the organs of vision in the human subject are—the *Hydatid* and the *Cysticercus telæ cellulosæ*, from amongst the class of cestoid worms; the *Monostomum lentis,* and *Distomum ophthalmobium,* belonging to the trematoda; and the *Filaria lentis,* and another species of Filaria, belonging to the nematoid class of entozoa.

With the exception of the cysticercus, all of these species have only been observed in a very small number of cases. The filaria lentis, the monostomum, and the distomum were found in the crystalline lens of patients suffering from cataract; the other filaria which was seen by Quadri, occurred in the anterior chamber of the eye; the hydatids were seen both in the anterior chamber, and in the deep-seated parts of the eye;[1] the cysticerci have been met with in most parts of the eye, with the exception of the lens.

The cysticerci have been more frequently observed in the deep-seated than in other parts of the eye, and, according to Graefe, who has recorded upwards of a dozen cases, they usually occupy the vitreous humour, the choroid membrane, or the retina. Their development is not generally attended with pain, although some patients have experienced a sense of pressure

---

[1] It has been suggested that the cases of hydatids stated by the earlier writers to have been observed in the anterior chamber of the eye were more probably cases of displacement of the lens, owing to rupture of its capsule. These cases are very doubtful, as the nature of the substance seen in the eye was not properly determined in any of them.

within the eyeball, and headache. Loss of vision comes on gradually until the sense of sight is at last completely destroyed. The iris sometimes changes its normal colour, but in the majority of cases no apparent alteration of the eye is perceptible; the other symptoms are similar to those which are present in all affections of the eye which are accompanied by dimness or loss of vision, and the aid of the ophthalmoscope is necessary in order to determine the existence of a cysticercus.

By means of this instrument, a small object may be seen, which is generally of a spherical shape, at least when the eye and the entozoon are quiescent, and of a bluish, greenish, or grey colour; its relation, with respect to the retinal vessels, varies according to the position which it occupies. When it is situated immediately in front of the retina, or in the vitreous humour, the retinal vessels do not pass in front of the object, but stop at its circumference, or are altogether invisible; but when the entozoon is lodged in the substance of the retina, or between this structure and those which are more deeply placed, the retinal vessels may be seen to ramify upon the object, or to run across it in order to divide further on, as in the healthy condition.

The tumour situated at the bottom of the eye is apparently formed by a cyst, whose delicately thin and transparent wall allows the entozoon to be seen, and its form and movements to be recognized. When the cysticercus is developed behind the retina, this structure is sometimes ulcerated, and the worm escapes into the vitreous humour. In some cases the cysticercus perishes, and becomes atrophied; Graefe mentions two cases of this kind, in which the eye was preserved, but the sight was lost.

Several cysticerci might exist at the same time in the vitreous humour, as has been observed in the pig.

One eye only is ordinarily affected, so that the prognosis would generally be more favourable than that of an ordinary attack of amaurosis; but the frequent multiplicity of cysticerci would warrant the apprehension, in some cases, that these entozoa were also present in the nervous centres.

Some benefit may be derived from an early operation, if the cysticercus can be extracted through the cornea. In one case, where Graefe made an opening through the cornea, and removed the cysticercus unbroken, the eye and sense of vision were both preserved; in others the sight was destroyed.

The entozoa which have been observed in the appendages of the eye are :—The trichina spiralis; the filaria Medinensis; the cysticercus telæ cellulosæ; hydatids; and a small nematoid worm, of uncertain species; this last was probably the Guinea-worm, although Guyot, who described this entozoon, states that the Guinea-worm is not found in Congo, where he observed it amongst the negroes. (See "Synopsis," p. 47).

The treatment of any of these entozoa would be similar to that of the same species, when they exist in the muscular, or in the areolar tissue, or beneath the integuments in other parts of the body.

PART III.

SPECIAL THERAPEUTICS.

ON THE VARIOUS MEDICINAL AGENTS EMPLOYED IN THE TREATMENT OF INTESTINAL AND OTHER ENTOZOA.

In the preceding chapters the plans of treatment for the different species of intestinal worms, and the best medicines which can be used for their expulsion, have been indicated ; but the remedies which have, from time to time, been employed have not been fully described. They will, therefore, be now discussed at greater length.

It would be useless to give an account of the anthelmintics which have received a trial at the hands of various observers ; as their number is very considerable, and the majority of them really possess no special vermifuge properties. Leclerc, in a work published at Geneva in 1715, furnishes a tabular statement of anthelmintics commonly known in his time ; of these, 379 remedies were obtained from the vegetable kingdom, 27 from the animal kingdom, and 13 from mineral substances. If all of the remedies which have, since that period, been tried and suggested, were enumerated, they would probably be found to amount to double the number mentioned by Leclerc.

Purgatives, and especially drastic purgatives, expel the worms by increasing the intestinal secretion, and by exciting the peristaltic movements of the intestine; they have for a long time constituted the principal medicines used in the treatment of intestinal entozoa, and they are frequently combined with substances which have a special vermifuge action.

The vermifuge remedies, that is to say, those which act upon the worms themselves, appear to do so, either by an actual poisonous effect upon the parasites, or by making their *habitat* offensive to them, as when assafœtida is administered, for instance.

The action of anthelmintics can only be correctly judged by observations of their effects upon man or upon animals. The trial of these remedies upon entozoa which have been removed from their natural habitat, cannot be depended upon, as they perish quickly, when they have arrived at the adult state, and it is difficult to estimate the relative share which the lowered temperature, the removal from their usual habitat, and the substance experimented with, have in causing the death of the worms. The numerous experiments which have been made by different observers are consequently of uncertain value.

The therapeutic agents which are used as anthelmintics do not possess an equal action upon all the intestinal entozoa, and most of them have a more marked influence upon certain species than upon others.

The following list, in which an alphabetical order

will be observed, includes the principal anthelmintic remedies; in some instances, the general description of one remedy may be considered as applicable to the others belonging to the same class; thus, Aloes may be regarded as representative of the anthelmintic action of purgatives.

Absinth.

The powder and infusion of the *Artemisia absinthium*, or common wormwood, have been long used in the treatment of intestinal entozoa. These preparations appear not only to exercise a poisonous influence upon the worms, but also to cause them to relax their hold upon the mucous membrane so that they are readily removed from the intestines by the subsequent administration of some purgative.

The species to which this plant belongs furnishes several other plants, possessing reputed vermifuge properties, of which the *A. santonicum* and *A. abrotanum*, are the chief. The natural order Compositæ, which comprises the Artemisiæ, also includes the chamomile, tansy, and other bitter herbs, which act similarly to, although not so efficaciously as, the wormwood.

The tonic properties of bitter preparations renders their employment serviceable after the expulsion of the entozoa by more powerful remedies, and their occasional administration is sometimes beneficial in keeping down the tendency to the development of intestinal worms.

Acids.

Most of the mineral acids have, at various times, been used in the diluted form, in the treat-

ment of intestinal entozoa, but their employment
does not seem to be attended by any marked results.
Professor Malmsten states that injections, acidulated
with nitric acid, were efficacious in destroying the
paramecia coli, observed by him in certain cases of
cholera and diarrhœa, and in checking the lienteric
diarrhœa which was produced by the irritation of
of these parasites. The other dilute mineral acids,
especially sulphuric, would probably fulfil the same
indications. Hydrocyanic acid has been recommended
by Brera, and other writers, to destroy the tænia
when it has been partly expelled from the intestines.

Aloes.

Aloes, gamboge, jalap, scammony, and other
purgatives were formerly the medicines most frequently resorted to in the treatment of intestinal
entozoa, both alone, and combined with other remedies. Their anthelmintic property is chiefly due to
their purgative effects; but aloes appears to possess
a special vermifuge action. Besides its internal use,
it is stated to have been employed with success
externally, in the form of poultices made of the fresh
juice of the plant, and applied to the abdomen; and
the instillation of tincture of aloes, combined with
one-half of its amount of water, between the eye-lids,
has been known to produce the death of filariæ,
which were situated in the anterior chamber of the
eye, and which became subsequently absorbed.

Antimonial Preparations.

During the last century tartarised antimony was largely employed as an anthelmintic, and
it has been strongly recommended for the treatment

of febrile affections produced by entozoa. When lumbrici get into the stomach, the vomiting caused by the administration of tartar emetic frees the patient of these troublesome parasites, and procures immediate relief. The expulsion of tænia has been accomplished by this remedy. An interesting case is quoted at page 109 of the successful injection of a solution of tartarised antimony into the veins, in a case of lumbrici, where the ordinary means of treatment could not be resorted to, owing to the rigid tetanic closure of the mouth and jaws.

Aspidium Filix Mas.

     The Aspidium Filix Mas, or Male Fern, is one of the most anciently known anthelmintics, having been used ·in the treatment of intestinal entozoa from the time of Galen and Dioscorides. Its efficacy is greatest in cases of bothriocephali and lumbrici ; when used for the purpose of expelling tænia, its action is not so well marked.

     Much of the disappointment and uncertainty which occur in the employment of anthelmintics, and other remedies taken from the vegetable kingdom, doubtless arises from the joint circumstances that the wrong plants are sometimes collected, that the parts which are used medicinally are gathered at an unsuitable season of the year, and that the dried plants or the preparations made from them are kept beyond the period during which they retain their active properties. ˙In some instances, also, as in that of santonine, for example, the high price which the drug commands in the market, unfortunately serves as an inducement to extensive adulterations.

The best season of the year for the collection of the root of the male fern, in which part of the plant the vermifuge properties are present, is the spring, according to Pescher, of Geneva, who has given much attention to this subject.

The forms in which this remedy are administered are various. Some practitioners give the powdered root made into an electuary with simple syrup; others prefer the etherial extract which, when fresh, is a very good preparation; Küchenmeister recommends some of the powdered root to be sprinkled over the extract, when it is taken, so as to increase the surface of contact of the medicine as much as possible. An extractive substance, filicine, or filicic acid, has been obtained from the plant, but it does not appear to possess any anthelmintic properties; and the infusion, decoction, and etherial oil, have also been prepared; the latter is highly spoken of, in the treatment of bothriocephali.

The dose of the extract is from a scruple to two drachms, of the powder from one to four drachms, and of the decoction from half an ounce to two ounces. The remedy should always be given in the morning, upon an empty stomach, and it should be followed in the course of an hour or two by a full dose of some purgative, castor-oil being one of the best.

The once-celebrated method of Nouffer, which was practised secretly for upwards of twenty years at Morat, in Switzerland, whither patients resorted in great numbers from all parts, and which was subsequently divulged upon the payment of eighteen thousand francs by the French government, in 1776,

consisted chiefly in the administration of three
drachms of the pulverised root in four ounces of the
infusion, and of a bolus composed of calomel, scammony, and gamboge after an interval of two hours.
When vomiting occurred, the remedy was repeated ;
and strong coffee was administered to prevent sickness. The dose was divided into two, or diminished
in quantity, for delicate adults and children. When
the bolus had failed in producing purgation within
four hours, or if the worm had not been wholly
expelled, it was usual to give to the patient an
ounce of the sulphate of magnesia dissolved in warm
water.

Anthelmintic properties have also been attributed
to another species of fern, the *Aspidium athamanticum,* which will be described under the head of
" *Panna.*"

Assafœtida.

This remedy has been long used in the
treatment of intestinal entozoa. It is almost inert
in the expulsion of the tænia, but it is sometimes
very serviceable, when given in the form of pills, in
cases of lumbrici, and when used in the form of
enemata, for the cure of oxyurides.

It undoubtedly exercises a valuable anthelmintic
action upon the worms which have their *habitat* in
the bronchial tubes of ruminant animals ; and it is
evident that, as it is taken into the stomach, it can
only act upon the entozoa situated in the air-passages through the medium of pulmonary absorption.
Recent experiments tend to prove that this medicinal
agent also expels the distoma from the biliary ducts ;

and in such cases, as also in those just mentioned, the assafœtida could only act by communicating to the secretions some peculiar quality which is obnoxious to the entozoa. An analogous property has been remarked when turpentine is administered. The worms are probably not destroyed; but they are compelled to abandon the various organs which have been rendered uninhabitable in consequence of the altered nature of the secretions. These facts give a strong semblance of probability to the statement which has been made respecting the Brahmins, namely, that they are protected from the attacks of the Guinea-worm, by their habitual use of assafœtida as an article of diet, although the other natives, who do not make the same free employment of this plant, are more or less affected by this parasite.

Garlic, onions, and other plants of a very strong, disagreeable odour, possess somewhat similar properties.

Camphor.

Camphor was held in great esteem as an anthelmintic, during the last century. Rœderer and Wagler gave it, in combination with purgatives, in the mucous epidemic, apparently due to the existence of worms in the intestines, which came under their notice. Rosen prescribed it in solution with vinegar; and Brera and Moscati directed their patients to take, at certain intervals, a spoonful of a mixture containing camphor and gum-arabic dissolved in water.

Some cases of tænia, in which the cure was attributed to the administration of camphor, have been

Q

recorded, and its solution would form a serviceable enema in cases of oxyurides ; but its effects are not sufficiently evident to admit of its being solely relied upon in the treatment of any species of entozoa.

Ether.

Sulphuric ether has been advantageously employed by several French practitioners in the treatment of oxyurides ; it is used in the form of an injection containing from half a drachm to two drachms of ether in solution in water. According to Compérat, this remedy possesses a double advantage, as it destroys the worms, and acts as a sedative in allaying the spasmodic and nervous complications caused by the irritation of the oxyurides in the rectum.

It has also been successfully administered, in the dose of a drachm in a glassful of the decoction of the male fern, for the expulsion of tænia.

Geoffreya.

The bark of the *Geoffreya Surinamensis* and of the *G. inermis* is much esteemed as a vermifuge in Surinam, where these two plants are indigenous. The fact of their properties, like those of many other exotic plants, being impaired after keeping for some time, has prevented their being extensively used in this country or on the continent ; the *G. inermis* is, however, included in the Dublin Pharmacopæia. The powdered bark may be given in half-drachm doses, in the form either of pills, or electuary; a decoction of it is occasionally employed.

Kamala.

This is a resinous substance obtained from the capsules of the fruit of the *Rottcria tinctoria*, a plant which grows in India, China, and other parts of Asia.

Dr. Mackinnon first directed attention to its value as an anthelmintic a few years since, in a paper in which he stated that its properties were well known to the natives of India; it was soon afterwards introduced into English practice,—Drs. Leared and Ramskill being amongst the first to pronounce favourably respecting its vermifuge properties,—and it is now looked upon as equal in efficacy and certainty of action to Kousso, and the other most highly esteemed anthelmintics. Its effects are best marked in cases of tænia and of lumbrici.

It may be given in the form of powder, in doses of one or two drachms, or of the tincture in two-drachm doses; four or six successive doses should be administered at intervals of four or five hours. It need not be so frequently repeated if the worm be expelled, or if there be much purging and griping pains in the bowels; the latter effects may be often obviated by the combination of hyoscyamus with the remedy, or by the administration of a small dose of castor oil. The tincture is superior to the powder, in consequence of its action being more certain, whilst it rarely produces severe nausea and colic.

Kousso.

The dried flowers of the Kousso, or *Brayera anthelmintica*, have been greatly extolled in the treatment of tænia and of bothriocephalus. This remedy has been commonly employed in Europe during the last twenty years only, although our celebrated countryman, James Bruce, made it known after his travels in Abyssinia. He called the plant, of which Kousso, or Cosso, is the native name, *Banksia Abyssinica*, in honour of Sir Joseph Banks, then President of the Royal Society; the more recent appellation, *Brayera anthelmintica*, was given to the plant in 1822, when Dr. Brayer, who had resided for several years in Turkey, brought some specimens of the Kousso to Paris.

The dose of the powdered Kousso is from two to six drachms; in larger quantities it produces sickness, violent cramps in the abdomen, and other unpleasant symptoms. Another great drawback in its administration, which induces many practitioners to give a preference to Kamala, is that it brings away the worm in pieces instead of expelling the whole of it at once, so that there is always a chance of the head remaining in the intestine. The odour and taste of Kousso form an obstacle to its administration to young children. The powdered Kousso ought to be given, as the infusion is not sufficiently powerful to expel the tænia; the dose may be divided, like that of other anthelmintics, into two or three portions, to be administered at frequent intervals, and it is advisable to give a dose of castor oil in about two or three hours after the last portion has been taken. The worm usually begins to come away, as is also the case when Kamala is employed, at about the third or fourth evacuation following the administration of the medicine.

Mechanical Irritants.

Under this head may be included the various substances which were formerly used in the treatment of intestinal worms, not on account of any specific vermifuge property which they possessed, but because they were supposed, by the penetration of their particles into the worms, to cause them to relax their hold upon the mucous membrane, so that they could be readily expelled by purgatives, administered subsequently.

The principal agents which were used with this view were the hairs of the pods of the *Dolichos pruriens*, or cowhage; steel, tin, and zinc, divided into minute, sharp spiculæ; and vegetable charcoal.

They were usually given in the form of an electuary, made by mixing the substance with simple syrup, honey, or treacle; and some purgative, generally castor oil, or a powder containing scammony, jalap, or calomel, was administered in the course of a few hours after the remedy had been taken.

They seldom failed to cause nausea, vomiting, colic, and severe intestinal irritation and inflammation, besides which they were often insufficient to procure the expulsion of the worms; so that they are now almost entirely abandoned.

Mulberry.

The bark of the root of this tree, *Morus nigra*, was formerly held in great repute as an anthelmintic, and was ranked by Galen and other old writers with the male fern and the pomegranate. It was principally used in the treatment of tænia. The dose of the powdered root is from one to four drachms; a decoction has also been prepared, but the extreme bitterness of this preparation renders the powder a preferable form for the administration of this remedy.

Musenna.

This is the bark of a leguminous plant, which grows upon the shores of the Red Sea. It is given in doses of from half an ounce to an ounce, or more, carefully powdered, and mixed with some semi-fluid vehicle, such as honey.

M. d'Abbadie, who has had numerous opportunities of observing the action of this remedy in the fresh state, considers it to be superior to Kousso, both in its anthelmintic property, and the fact that musenna does not produce any marked disturbance of the digestive functions, like Kousso does. He also remarks that musenna should be given about two or three hours before a meal, and that the tænia is usually expelled upon the following day, without the occurrence of severe purging, or of colic.

Owing to its losing its vermifuge property through being kept, its administration in Europe has not been attended by such results as would lead to its adoption in preference to some of the other anthelmintics in ordinary use.

Nitrate of Silver.

Injections of water containing nitrate of silver, in solution, in the proportion of about two grains to one ounce of water, have been favourably spoken of by Schultze, of Daidesheim, in the treatment of oxyurides. The first enema is commonly passed out of the bowels soon after its injection, together with dead or dying oxyurides; the repetition of the enemata upon two or three occasions usually suffices for the entire destruction of the parasites, according to the author just mentioned.

Panna.

This is a species of fern (the *Aspidium athamanticum*), which is indigenous to Southern Africa; its root is employed by the Kaffirs for the purpose of expelling the tænia.

Dr. Behrens, in a paper published in the *Deutsche Klinik* for 1856, states that he has found it successful in procuring the expulsion of tænia.

The patient should be placed upon a low diet for a few days before the administration of the remedy, and the powdered root is to be then given in doses of a scruple or a scruple and a half in a little water, repeated every quarter of an hour until three or four doses have been administered; a dose of castor oil should be given at about two hours after the last dose of the *panna*.

This remedy sometimes causes sickness, or temporary headache, but it never gives rise to any serious complications.

Papaya.

The *Carica papaya* is a tree which is found in the West Indies; its stem furnishes a milky juice of a bitter taste, and very abundant in coagulable azotised matter.

This juice has been very favourably mentioned by various writers, as an anthelmintic, its efficacy being most marked in the treatment of lumbrici. Dyer, in a paper in the *London Medical Gazette* for 1834, states that it is largely employed in the Mauritius, and that it is an excellent vermifuge, and exempt from any risk to the patient, even when it is given in full doses. It is unfortunately difficult to keep, and consequently loses much of its valuable properties when imported to Europe.

Pomegranate.

The bark of the root of this plant has long been acknowledged to possess valuable anthelmintic properties. Both the wild and the cultivated pomegranate are used indiscriminately; the vermifuge action of the root is in a direct ratio to the freshness of the specimen which is employed.

When it is administered in the form of powder, the dose is from half a drachm to two or three drachms; the decoction, which is considered by some to be a better form of administering this drug, is given in doses of half an ounce to two ounces. Its administration is not followed by any bad complications; the majority of the patients do not experience any ill effects, but sometimes a portion of the medicine is rejected, or there may be simple nausea, when the stomach is more than ordinarily sensitive; colic, flatulency, purging, and vertigo have occasionally been induced by the use of this remedy, but they soon pass off.

The tænia is generally expelled about six hours after the administration of the pomegranate root, which is equally efficacious in the destruction of the bothriocephalus.

Pumpkin.

The seeds of the pumpkin and gourd were recommended as early as 1683 by our countryman, E. Tyson, for the treatment of tænia. This remedy subsequently fell into disuse, but it has been recently introduced again into practice by Cazin, Tarneau, and other French medical men, who state that its anthelmintic effects are very decided.

The method in which the seeds are prepared for use is by removing the husks, and then making the seeds into an electuary by bruising them in a mortar, and afterwards mixing them with sugar and milk.

The dose in which they should be given is from half an ounce to two ounces ; and in order that the full benefit should be obtained, it is requisite that they should be given when the patient is fasting, and that some castor oil should be administered in about two or three hours after they have been taken. This remedy is said to possess the advantage of occasioning neither nausea nor colic.

Salt.

A solution of salt, used as an enema, furnishes an excellent means of promptly expelling oxyurides from the rectum or vagina; and, if repeated on several successive days, it sometimes effects a complete cure.

Salt has also been administered internally for the cure of tænia, in the dose of a teaspoonful dissolved in a glass of water, night and morning ; the quantity being gradually increased.

Santonine.

The anthelmintic properties of the different

species of *Artemisia*, especially of the *A. abrotanum* and *A. santonicum*, were very generally recognised amongst the ancients, as may be deduced from the circumstance that we find a recommendation of them for the treatment of intestinal worms in the works of Paulus Ægineta, Dioscorides, Galen, Celsus, and other early medical writers; and the use of these remedial agents has been continued, in various forms, up to the present time. In France and other continental countries extensive recourse has long been had, when a vermifuge was required, to the administration of wormseed, also known by the abbreviated name of " semen-contra " (*i. e., semen contra vermes*), which consists of the broken flower-stalks, involucres, and flower-buds of several kinds of *Artemisia*. The chief objection to the use of this remedy is that the large quantity—nearly half-an-ounce—given as a dose is apt to produce dyspepsia and sickness, and it has consequently been abandoned in great measure for santonine, a crystalline substance, which is procured from wormseed, and which possesses similar properties.

Santonine, or cinine, as it is sometimes called, is a white, inodorous, and, when pure, almost tasteless powder; very sparingly soluble in water, but readily dissolved in fatty oils. It has a slightly acid reaction, of which advantage has been taken in the manufacture of a series of salts, santonates, formed by its union with certain bases.[1]

For children, one to three grains would constitute

---

[1] The principal of these salts, the santonate of soda, is given in doses of from five to eight grains for adults, and from two to four grains for children.

a proper dose, and for adults, two to five grains administered twice daily; the remedy may be repeated every third or fourth day, for one or more successive weeks, if necessary. It should be given in some oily vehicle, and none will be found more advantageous than castor oil. If, for any reason, castor oil be unsuitable, the powdered santonine may be given on a piece of bread and butter, or in honey, some purgative, such as jalap, being ordered to be taken about three hours afterwards. When the ascaris oxyuris is the parasite with which the patient is troubled, some of the drug may be combined with an enema.

I have, for some years past, employed santonine, both in Hospital and private practice, in a considerable number of cases, from which I propose to give a summary of fifty, in order to show the value of that remedy.

In twenty-eight of these cases the prevailing entozoon was the ascaris oxyuris, in seventeen the tænia solium, and in five the ascaris lumbricoides. Of the total number of patients nineteen were cured after undergoing treatment for a duration of from one to three weeks, fifteen were much relieved, nine presented some improvement, and in the remaining seven no permanent good result was obtained.

The relative efficacy of the medicine varies according to the species of parasite, the greatest degree of benefit being procurable in the cases of round-worm, next in tape-worm, and least in those of the thread-worm; this comparison only holds good, however, when the santonine is administered by the mouth, for the cure effected by the use of enemata containing santonine is sometimes very speedy in cases of thread-worm.

Some authors have raised an objection to the use of santonine, in consequence of certain secondary results which are occasionally produced by it, of which the most common is the peculiar coloration of the vision, everything appearing to the patient to be of a yellow or greenish tint. This phenomenon is only of a transient character, and passes off in a few hours after the suspension of the drug, or sooner if a purgative be administered, without causing any injury ; but it would always, of course, be proper to apprise the patient of its possible occurrence.

Various conjectural explanations of this singular phenomenon have been offered ; some have attempted to account for it by supposing that the serum of the blood acquires a yellowish tinge ; and others, again, imagine that a temporary influence is exerted upon the optic nerve, or the retina. Its coincidence with the exhibition of santonine internally has, as might be expected, induced some practitioners to give that agent a trial in the treatment of deeply-seated affections of the eye. Dr. Martini, of Naples, has reported that much benefit attended its adminis- tration in several cases of nervous amaurosis ; and M. Guépin, of Nantes, has confirmed Dr. Martini's statements ; but further evidence of the nature and degree of the action of santonine upon the visual organs is necessary before it can be admitted into the list of acknowledged ophthalmic remedies.

The preceding remarks formed part of a paper of of mine on this subject which was inserted in the *Medical Times and Gazette*, for 1862. The results which I have observed, both in my published and unpublished cases, incline me to the opinion that santonine is one of the most perfect anthelmintics which we at present possess, seeing that it combines the advantage of smallness of bulk, as regards the dose in which it is taken, and of absence of unpleasant taste, or serious complications, with considerable certainty of action. The high price which santonine commands, unfortunately leads to great and frequent adulterations of this drug, to which I believe that the disappointment complained of by many in the results procured by the administration of santonine is chiefly due.

Saoria.

This is the fruit of the *Mæsa picta,* an Abyssinian plant, and is used by the natives as an anthelmintic, both in the fresh and in the dried state.

When dried, it is given in one ounce doses, powdered, and mixed with a quantity of gruel. Schimper says that it produces purging, and expels the tænia dead and whole, without the risk of the injury to the patient's health, which occasionally follows the administration of Kousso. Although its efficacy is most shown in cases of tænia, it is deserving of a trial in the treatment of lumbrici and oxyurides.

It has been tried by several European medical practitioners, and Strohl, of Strasburg, speaks very favourably of it, in some cases of tænia, which he treated with this remedy. The chief objection to its use is that, although the body of the worm is expelled, the head is usually left behind ; castor oil should consequently be always given in full doses after the administration of the Saoria.

It has a peculiar effect upon the urine, to which it imparts a violet colour.

Spigelia Marilandica.

This is a perennial herbaceous plant, indigenous to North America, where it is known by the common name of the Carolina Pink. The root, which is the part used medicinally, consists of a number of slender, blackish fibres.

Although it has been omitted from the recent editions of the London Pharmacopæia, it is held in great esteem in America, where it is employed more frequently, perhaps, than any other anthelmintic ; it is especially efficacious in the treatment of lumbrici.

It may be given in the form either of the powdered root, or the decoction, the dose of the root being from ten grains to a scruple, two or three times daily. Some purgative should be administered after it ; or, when it is given in the form of decoction, senna leaves may be added to the preparation. A fluid extract, which is of uncertain value, is sometimes given in doses of from half a drachm to two drachms.

Sulphur.

This substance was formerly prescribed in the treatment of lumbrici and of oxyurides, but its use internally, as an anthelmintic, is now discontinued.

According to Lallemand, sulphuretted water, employed in the form of an enema, is an excellent remedy for oxyurides ; the injection should be cold.

Tatzé.

The fruit called Tatzé, or Zatzé, is obtained from a plant which grows in Abyssinia, at the Cape of Good Hope, in Algeria, and some other parts of Africa.

It is used in the treatment of tænia, and is very similar in its effects, to Kousso and Saoria ; but it is said to be more apt to produce vomiting and colic than the latter remedy.

The dose in which it is given is from two to six drachms, powdered and dissolved in water.

Turpentine.

The oil of turpentine is very efficacious in the treatment of tænia, and, were it not for the distressing complications often produced by it, would be one of the best anthelmintics.

It should be administered in the morning, whilst the patient is fasting, in doses of from two drachms to an ounce and a half, and castor oil should be given in combination with it, or within the space of about two hours after the administration of the turpentine. The patient should not be allowed to drink any fluid until the medicine has operated, lest nausea and sickness should be induced.

In the majority of cases, the oil of turpentine gives rise to severe vomiting, strangury, headache, and a species of intoxication. The bowels ought always to be kept freely open by the administration of castor oil until the peculiar violet-like odour of the urine, which is indicative of the presence of the oil of turpentine in the circulation, has completely disappeared.

The once-famous empyreumatic preparation, called Chabert's oil, after its inventor, Chabert, a veterinary surgeon of considerable skill, and author of a work entitled *Traité des maladies vermineuses dans les animaux*, published in 1782, consists of three parts of oil of turpentine, and one part of oil of hartshorn. It is exceedingly nauseous, besides being tedious and unsafe in its action, so that it is now seldom used in the treatment of entozoa in the human subject, although it is much employed on the continent as an anthelmintic for cattle.

Varec.

The Varec, or Corsican Moss, is a remedy commonly used in France, and consists of a mixture of several species of Algæ. The *Fucus helmintho-corton* forms about a third of this mixture, the rest being composed of different plants, including the *Corallina officinalis*. The latter is sometimes used alone, but its anthelmintic property is not so strongly marked as that of the *Fucus helminthocorton*.

Varec is given either in the form of decoction, or of the powdered substance, of which from fifteen grains to a drachm forms the ordinary dose; it is repeated for several successive days, and, like all anthelmintics, should be administered in the morning, before the patient has taken any food.

It is most efficacious in the treatment of lumbrici, but, owing to its frequent adulteration, it is of very uncertain value.

GLOSSARY

PRINCIPAL TERMS USED IN THE SYNOPSIS.

***

ACANTHOTHECA. (Ἄκανθα, a thorn, a prickle, and θήκη, a covering.) One of the classes of entozoa has received this name, in consequence of the numerous little projections with which the bodies of the worms comprised in it are covered.

ACEPHALOCYST. (A, not; κεφαλή, a head; and κύστις, a bladder.) The headless hydatid, which presents a bladder-like appearance.

ACULEATUS. (*Aculeus*, a prickle.) This term has been given to a species of Dactylius, which was once observed in the urine by Mr. Curling, and which has a number of sharp spinous processes upon its integument.

ALATA. (*Alatus*, winged.) A term applied by Bellingham to a a species of Ascaris which is furnished with two wing-like expansions near the head.

ALTRICIPARIENS. (*Vide* SCOLICIPARIENS.)

ANCHYLOSTOMUM. (Ἀγκύλη, a contraction, and στόμα, the mouth.) A genus of nematoid worm, in which the anterior part of the body is contracted.

ASCARIS. (Σκαίρω, to move quickly.) A genus of the nematoid worms.

BACTERIUM. (Βακτήριον, from βαίνω, to move about.) One of the genera of the Protozoa.

BOTHRIOCEPHALUS. (Βόθριον, a trench or groove, and κεφαλή, a head.) A genus of the cestoid entozoa, which has two lateral, longitudinal grooves upon its head.

CERCARIA. (Κέρκος, a tail, and ἀρίς, a file.) This name has been given to the larva of the distomum, which is furnished, during the earlier portion of its existence, with a tail, and which is able, by the aid of its buccal apparatus, to penetrate the integuments of certain animals.

CERCOMONAS. (Κέρκος, and μονάς, a single point.) This is a minute animalcule, which differs from the *monas*, in the circumstance of its possessing a caudal prolongation.

CESTOIDEA. (Κεστός, shaped like a flat band, and εἶδος, a resemblance.) An important class of the entozoa, in which the long ribbon-like worms are included.

CŒNURUS. (Κοινός, common, and οὐρά, a tail.) A genus of cestoid worm, characterised by a vesicle, common to several bodies, each of which is terminated by a head provided with four suckers, above which is arranged a double crown of hooklets. This genus is peculiar to herbivorous animals.

CRASSICOLLIS. (*Crassus*, thick, and *collum*, the neck.) A species of Tænia, *T. crassicollis*, is found in the cat and other feline animals.

CUCURBITINUS. (*Cucurbita*, a gourd.) The rings of the tænia have some resemblance to the seeds of the gourd, and consequently received the name of *cucurbitini* from the older writers.

CYSTICERCUS. (Κύστις, a bladder, and κέρκος, a tail.) A genus of the cestoid entozoa, remarkable for the caudal vesicle which the worms in this genus possess.

DACTYLIUS. (Δακτύλιος, a ring.) A genus of the nematoid worms.

DENTICOLA. (*Dens;* genitive *dentis*, a tooth, and *colo*, to inhabit.) An infusorial parasite, which lives in the matter which collects about the teeth.

DIBOTHRIUS. (Δìς, twice, and βοθριον, a groove.) Another name for the Bothriocephalus.

DICYSTUS. (Δìς, and κύστις, a bladder.) A variety of Cysticercus, consisting of two vesicles.

DIGENESIS. (Δìς, and γένεσις, origin.) The transition through two distinct stages of development.

DISTOMUM. (Δìς, and στόμα, a mouth.) The entozoa in the genus *Distomum* possess two mouths, or suckers.

DRACUNCULUS. (*Dracunculus*, the diminitive of *draco*, a serpent.) One of the former names of the Guinea-worm.

ECHINOCOCCUS. ('Εχῖνος, beset with prickles, and κόκκος, a berry.) A species of immature tænia.

ENTOZOA. ('Εντὸς, within, and ζῶον, an animal.) Animals which live within the organs of other animals.

FILARIA. (*Filum*, a thread) A genus of the nematoid entozoa.

GEMMATION. (*Gemma*, a bud.) The act of growing by means of buds, or germs.

GYNŒCOPHORUS. (Γυνὴ, a female, and φέρω, to bear.) The term applied to the canal, *Canalis gynæcophorus*, within which the female of the *distomum hæmatobium* is contained.

HAMULARIA. (*Hamulus*, a hook.) A species of Filaria, so named in consequence of the two projecting hooks which are situated upon its under surface.

HÆMATOBIUM. (Αἷμα, blood, and βιόω, to live.) A species of Distomum (the D. hæmatobium) found in the portal vein and its tributaries.

HETEROPHYES. (Ἕτερος, another, different, and φύω, to produce.) A species of Distomum (the D. heterophyes) which differs in appearance from the other species.

HEXACANTHUS. (Ἕξ, six, and ἄκανθα, a prickle.) The six-hooked embryo of the Tænia.

HOLOSTOMUM. (Ὅλος, the whole, entire, and στόμα, the mouth.) A genus of the nematoid entozoa.

HYDATID. (Ὑδατὶς, a vesicle.) A genus of the Cestoidea, principally composed of a membrane containing a watery fluid.

HYDATIGENA. (Ὑδατὶς, and γίγνομαι, to be born.) Proceeding from a hydatid.

INERMIS. (*Inermis*, unarmed.) A variety of the Tænia, which is not furnished with hooklets upon the head, whence its distinctive name (T. inermis).

INFUSORIA. (*Infusum*, an infusion.) Belonging to infusions. A class which comprises the minute animalcules, which exist in various infusions, in stagnant water, &c.

LANCEOLATUM. (*Lanceolatus*, having the shape of a spear.) A term applied to a species of Distomum (D. lanceolatum).

LONGEVAGINATUS. (*Longevaginatus*, having a long sheath). A designation given to a species of Strongylus (S. longevaginatus).

MONAS. (Μονὰς, a single point.) A species of infusorial worm.

MONOGENESIS. (Μόνος, single, and γένεσις, origin.) The transition through a single state of development only.

MONOSTOMUM. (Μόνος, single, and στόμα, the mouth.) A species of trematode worm which possesses one sucker only.

MYSTAX. (Μύσταξ, the upper lip.) A term applied to a species of Ascaris (the A. mystax), found in the cat and some other animals. The name is given in consequence of the membranous expansions near the mouth.

NANA. (*Nanus*, a dwarf.) This term is applied to the smallest of the Tæniæ (T. nana).

NEMATOID. (Νῆμα, a thread, and εἶδος, a resemblance.) A class of entozoa, in which the long, filiform worms are included.

OPHTHALMOBIUM. ('Οφθαλμος, the eye, and βιόω, to live.) The D. ophthalmobium is a small trematode worm which has been observed in the interior of the eye.

OXYURIS. ('Οξύς, sharp, and οὐρά, the tail.) A species of nematoid worm, in which the body tapers off gradually at the posterior portion.

PARAMECIUM. (Παρά, amongst, μήκων, excrementitious matter.) An infusorial worm, which is sometimes observed in the evacuations, or in the contents of the colon.

PENTASTOMUM. (Πέντε, five, στόμα, the mouth.) The parasites included in the genus Pentastomum have four cavities, into which the hooks can be retracted, situated near the mouth, so that they possess altogether five mouth-like openings, from which peculiarity the name of the genus is derived.

POLYSTOMUM. (Πολύς, many, and στόμα.) Under the head of Polystoma, or Polystomata, are included all the trematode worms which are provided with more than two suckers.

POLYMORPHUS. (Πολύς, many, and μορφή, shape.) Having many forms, or shapes.

PROSCOLEX. (Πρό, before, σκώληξ, a worm.) The phase of development which immediately precedes the scolex.

PROTOZOA (Πρῶτος, first, ζῶον, a living animal.) Under this head are included the first, or simplest, forms of living organization.

ROSTRUM. (*Rostrum*, a beak.) This term is applied to the projection which exists upon the head, in some of the cestoid worms.

SCOLEX. (Σκώληξ, a worm.) This word is used to designate a phase of development of the cestoid entozoa.

SCOLICIPARIENS. (Σκώληξ, and *pario*, to bring forth.) A term applied by Küchenmeister to the *Echinococcus Veterinorum*, i. e., the Echinococcus found in animals, as distinguished from the *E. hominis*, found in man, to which that writer has given the name *E. altriciipariens* (from *alter*, another, and *pario*, to bring forth).

SERRATA. (*Serratus*, notched.) The *tænia serrata*, very common in the small intestine of the dog, has a number of projections, resembling the teeth of a saw, arranged along its two margins, whence this species derives its distinctive name.

SPIROPTERA. (*Spira*, a convolution, and πτερὰ, a wing.) A nematoid worm, which has received this name in consequence of the spiral tail of the male, furnished with membranous wing-like expansions.

SPOROCYST. (Σπορὰ, a seed, a germ cell, and κύστις, a bladder.) The second phase in the development of a distomum.

STROBILE. (*Strobilus*, a cone.) A phrase employed to designate the body of a cestoid worm.

STRONGYLUS. (Στρογγύλος, round, cylindrical.) A genus of the nematoid entozoa. The only species, of which the existence has been fully ascertained in man, is of very considerable size, whence it has received the name of *S. gigas*.

TÆNIA. (Ταινία, a band.) The tape-worm.

TRACHELOCAMPHYLUS. (Τράχηλος, the neck, and καμπύλος, bent, curved.) One of the varieties of cysticercus.

TREMATODA. (Τρῆμα, a cavity; εἶδος, a resemblance.) The trematode class of entozoa derives its name from the existence of one or more depressions, which serve as organs of adherence.

TRICHINA. (Θρίξ, genitive τριχὸς, a hair.) A small nematoid worm, found in the muscles.

TRICHOMONAS. (Θρίξ, genitive τριχὸς, and μονὰς, a single point.) One of the genera of the Protozoa.

TRICOCEPHALUS. (Θρίξ, genitive τριχὸς, and κεφαλὴ, the head.) The entozoon to which this name is applied is smaller at the anterior than at the posterior portion; at one time the smaller end was supposed to be the tail of the worm, so that it was then called the *Trichuris* (from Θρίξ, genitive τριχὸς, and οὐρὰ, the tail).

VIBRIO. (*Vibro*, to shake.) The animalcules included in the genus Vibrio are capable of executing rapid movements by means of repeated vibrations.

INDEX.

THE END.